HIS LITTLE RED

Mayhem Ever After Series

VIVI PAIGE

Blurb

I stole her from her life.

I'll go even further to keep her in mine.

She was a job. Nothing more. Nothing less.

I took her from the party. It wasn't personal. It was a contract.

Grab her, head to the safehouse, and wait for the ransom.

Scarlett is so gentle, so trusting.

She doesn't know that men like me exist.

Doesn't know the brutal nature of this world.

Me? I come from a world of violence.

I'm a killer. I prey on nightmares and make them come true.

If you cross me, I kill you.

So when her father decided not to pay, word comes down that I'm supposed to torture her.

If he still doesn't cough up the cash, I'm supposed to kill her.

I won't hurt this fiery angel.

I crave her.

Me, a monster that could never be what she needs.

Who can never settle down.

I can't just do the job and destroy her.

No, I have to make her mine. Forever.

The way this thing is going down… it's going to be either her love.

Or her life.

Welcome to Mayhem Ever After series! This is the first in a series of dark, possessive, alpha male romances featuring brooding heroes and the sassy women that love them. No cheating. No cliffhangers. HEA guaranteed!

Chapter One

Will

A RESOUNDING *CRACK* ECHOED THROUGH THE DIVE BAR, *Stripes*, as I smashed the cue ball in the sweet spot. Like a whirling dervish, it shot toward the racked colored balls, and a duller yet more intense *crack* echoed through the smoky air. Cigars and cigarettes still flew here, in blatant defiance of clean air laws. The type of clientele *Stripes* tended to attract—ex-service men and women—weren't the type to call the state health department in a tizzy, so it was a pretty low-risk affair.

I grinned in satisfaction as I beheld the fruits of my labors. My erstwhile companions, however, were less enthusiastic. Particularly, my opponent in this game of pool.

"Aw, man, look at that break," Jon scowled as four of the stripes sank into the pockets but none of the solids. "Fucking sharking me, man."

"Why would I do that, Jon-boy?" I smirked and lined up my next shot. "You don't have any money. Obviously, I'm stripes."

"Yeah, obviously." Jon chuckled. "I suppose I should be grateful you're picking up the tab."

Stripes wasn't an overly large joint. Less than a dozen patrons were usually here at a time and it got to feeling crowded. But it was a great place to shoot pool without some broflake trying to hustle a guy. The low ceiling and pseudo-military aesthetic weren't exactly my jam, but I was there to shoot pool and throw back some brews, not admire the scenery.

And speaking of admiring the scenery… Janie the barmaid kept flashing smiles my way. At five foot, one inch of pure stacked blonde sexiness, Janie was considered a prize by my fellows, but I'd already tapped that once. So, I just nodded when she looked my way. Didn't even smile.

"Dude," Steve, Jon's cousin and one of the guys we suffered through basic with, spoke up. His speech was slurred since he'd gotten a head start on happy hour. His apartment was a short walk away, so as long as he could stumble down the sidewalk without getting picked up for public intoxication, I guess he was all right. "Janie keeps checking you out, Wolf. How are you not all over that shit?"

Jon laughed as I missed my shot and cursed my luck. "Didn't you hear? Will already took her home last week. You know he's not into repeat performances."

"Damn straight," Steve drawled, watching Jon attempt an ill-conceived masse shot. "If I had shoulders and abs like that, I'd probably be rolling in pussy, too."

I shrugged because I was hardly rolling in pussy, as he so quaintly put it. Did I lack for female company? No, but I also wasn't a hound dog whose only interest was getting laid. You know, like those two idiots.

"Still, man, just because you fucked her once doesn't mean you can't dip your cock in it again." Steve clapped me on the shoulder as Jon missed a shot. "Come on, man, we want to live vigorously through you."

"I think you mean vicariously, Steve-O," I grunted. "And you'll have to find someone else to perform that particular service."

"Vicar-whaterously?" Steve flashed me a confused frown.

"You know rich boy here went to the finest private schools before he enlisted with us schmucks, right?" Jon straightened. "You didn't leave me with any decent shots, you bastard."

"Why should I leave you with any decent shots?" I mused with a grin as I lined up my next point of attack.

"Why did a rich guy like you join the Army, anyway?" Steve asked. "You want to prove you're a tough guy?"

"Something like that." I smashed the cue ball and sank another stripe.

"Bullshit," Jon leaned over the table and grinned. "You joined the Army because your girlfriend picked big brother over you."

"What? For real?" Steve cackled way too damned loud.

My face twisted up in a grimace. Obviously, it wasn't a memory I savored with any degree of relish. It's quite unusual for someone from my affluent background to go through basic training. ROTC—that's Reserve Officers' Training Corps to civvies—or a fancy academy like West Point were more appropriate. But I wanted out of my household, fast, and had no time for wait lists or favors to come through.

"Shut up, Jon," I sighed. "You're breaking my concentration."

"Yeah, for real." Jon ignored the fact I'd spoken. "You were just too wasted to remember the time he broke down in tears during basic and whined about her."

I know Jon didn't mean any malice by what he said. He was just trying to blow my concentration.

I still made my shot.

"Eight ball, side pocket." I tapped the appropriate hole with the end of the cue.

"You're going to miss, dumb ass," Jon growled as I lined up my shot. "Miss, miss, miss…"

Crack. The eight ball sank like a stone while the cue ball rolled back to bounce harmlessly off the bumper. Just the way I'd planned. The thing about pool was that it was a game of seeming dichotomies. In order to hit ball A with ball B, one may not wish to directly strike at the target at all. This was where banked shots came in. I'd never been a pool shark, my companion's statements notwithstanding, but I'd always excelled at picking my shots. I'd tried to apply that concept in all avenues of my life outside the world of felt-covered marble.

"Fucking A, man," Jon sighed. "Best five out of seven?"

"Fuck a B, there's more holes," Steve slurred. "No more chances, cuz. It's my turn to face off against Mr. Lone Wolf here before big bro comes and tosses a leash on him."

Looking back, I'm not sure what tipped me off to my brother's presence before he even came in the door. Maybe there's some underlying empathetic connection between brothers, or maybe it was because Jon talked about the bastard. For whatever reason, I was already looking at the front door of *Stripes* when in sauntered Devlin.

Devlin's my older brother, with the same wavy black hair and blue eyes as me. He's a bit slimmer, especially across the shoulders, but I've wrestled him enough to know he possesses a wiry strength, which belies his slender frame. Unlike me, who prefers jeans and t-shirts most of the time, he always dresses to the nines. That day was no exception, with a black Ralph Lauren blazer over an ivory button-up shirt, which complemented his charcoal slacks. Shiny Bruno Maglis adorned his feet, as if he didn't already seem quite out of place in a dive like *Stripes*.

Our eyes met, and he crossed the room, his nose wrinkled in disgust. His flashy shoes clunked off the uneven wooden floor, crunching down on peanut shells with a note of finality.

"What is that smell?" Devlin held a handkerchief over his mouth and nose.

"Probably Chet's pork burger meat," Jon offered. "He marinates it for hours and it gets pretty intense. Guess we're all used to the smell."

Devlin looked at Jon but did not speak to him. In Devlin's mind, Jon was low class. It was my business to slum it, but Devlin wasn't about to join in the fun.

"I need to speak with you, Will." Devlin, always cryptic. He had that particular tone that let me know right away it was business. *Firm* business.

Legally, we're a security consulting firm, which brings in a fair amount of profit—say, thirty percent of our take, and one hundred percent of what we report to the Feds. Unofficially, we're the guys who are called when the shit hits the fan and everyone wants Johnny Law to stay completely unaware—most importantly, uninvolved. I guess some could call us the bad guys. We're definitely skirting and sometimes outright breaking the law, but from what I've seen, there is no such thing as black and white morality. Everything is shades of gray, and I know my gray is more muted than most.

"I'll be back in a bit, boys." I grabbed my phone off the edge of the pool table and followed Devlin back out into the sunlight. His limo sat nearby, wildly out of place in the street-level environs.

We climbed into the back, me ducking my head low to fit through the door.

Devlin clambered in after me, and as soon as the door shut, he sighed. "Will, what's the point of having a cell phone if you never answer it?"

"I answer it most of the time. I'm off duty, Devlin."

"You're never off duty from the firm," Devlin snapped.

"Whatever. Just tell me what's so important you couldn't let me finish my pool game."

"Hmph." Devlin handed me a lumpy manila envelope. I could tell by the feel that there was a burner cell phone inside along with some documents.

"So who needs a dirt nap?" I opened the envelope.

"No one," Devlin answered. "It's a collection and babysitting gig."

Devlin meant a kidnapping, but even when we're pretty damn certain no one's listening in, we use euphemisms. It's a habit drilled into us ever since we were young. I have memories from when I was fourteen of being forced to eat a bar of soap for talking too boldly about company business in my father's office.

I tilted the envelope so the contents would slide out onto the plush leather seat beside me. The expected phone plopped out, as well as several pages of photos, obviously printed out from a computer rather than professionally developed.

I glanced at the pics and then refocused on my brother. "I don't do jobs involving women or children, Devlin." I stonily handed him the phone. "I've been very clear about this. *Very* clear."

The photos all depicted a gorgeous twenty-something woman with red wavy hair down to her shoulders and bright, intelligent eyes that seem to hint at an inner toughness.

I'd do her, I thought, as a bulge grew in my jeans. *I'd do her hard.*

"Calm down, Will," Devlin rolled his eyes and forced the phone back into my hand. "She's not going to get hurt. Once the drop off is made, she gets to walk off without a scratch."

"And if there's no drop off?"

"Then you do what you gotta do to make sure there is."

"I don't like this." I stuffed the items back into the envelope. "Not one bit."

"You don't have to like it, baby bro," Devlin sneered. "When you walked away from the firm—from the family—that was supposed to be it. No second chances, no welcoming you back into the fold. You went and fought and bled for Uncle Sam and left us in the lurch. Now, you're back and you want in."

"Seriously, Devlin?" I arched an eyebrow and an old sting returned to the surface. "After the role you played in my leaving the firm, you're going to say something like that?"

"Hey, Lily made her own choices, Will." Devlin shrugged, and I could tell he was trying hard to be nice about the situation. As nice as he got, anyway. "I didn't seduce her. She seduced me. If you really cared about her, you would try and respect her choices. Besides, this isn't about the past. It's about your future with the firm. You need to prove you're still loyal to us first and foremost. Family is everything."

I only hesitated a moment before bumping his offered fist.

"Family is everything," I agreed. "I'll do it. Do you have a name to go along with the photos? Or do I have to do my own legwork on this one?"

"You're looking at Scarlett Shaw, eldest daughter of Hunter Shaw. You ever heard of him?"

"The gun guy?" I scratched my head. "I think so, but I never knew he had a daughter."

Especially not one who looked like that. Just my type.

Just.

My.

Type.

"Well, he does, and he's loaded, so we're sending her on a little vacation until Daddy pays up. I'll leave the details in your capable hands, and we'll keep in touch."

I exited the limo, envelope clutched in my hand. It looked like shooting the shit time tonight was at an end. I wished I didn't have an ominous gut feeling about the op.

Chapter Two

Scarlett

THE SUN BROKE THROUGH THE GRIM GRAYNESS OF thunder clouds, lancing bright beams of golden sunlight over the Big Apple's rain-soaked streets. Finally. I'd been waiting for the cloud cover to break for what seemed like ages.

Of course, there were worse places to wait out the rain than *Rainbow*, the influencer-friendly café about two blocks from Times Square. They had booths designed specifically for podcasters and vloggers, and my favorite feature—a picture window with a great view of the New York skyline.

I'd been waiting for the clouds to break so I could have a better background for my latest podcast. My notes sat neatly stacked on the polished table and my pink-cased digital camera sat on the tripod just awaiting my order to begin filming.

"Hey, how's that latte treating you?"

I turned my gaze away from my notes to the male barista hovering over me. He wasn't bad looking, not at all. Chiseled cheekbones, in good shape with a narrow waist and nice muscle tone. However, the man bun was a major turn-off. I knew my ideology tended to attract the "wheatgrass bros" like light attracted moths, but that didn't mean I was happy about the experience.

I was the kind of woman who preferred a manly man. One who didn't wax his chest hair, wear a man bun, or count carbs—a real caveman type. But those types tended to be the kind of folks who out and out hated my podcasts. "There goes the liberal hippie commie pinko girl again, trying to take away our guns."

Muh rights. Muh freedoms. *Please.*

"It's fine, thank you," I smiled sweetly. It was the third time that guy had checked on me that afternoon. I wasn't dressed especially flirty at the time—a tight black sweater and gray skirt with opaque stockings just in case I forgot to keep my legs crossed during filming. No way did I want to end up one of those panty flashing memes.

"Are you finally going to start your podcast?" He refused to take the hint and scram. "The one about the guns?"

"The one about gun control," I corrected him.

"Great." He stood there, waiting for me to elaborate or give him more attention, but I pored over my notes instead. Not that he gave up so easily. "So, you need some more skyjuice?"

I lifted my gaze to him, ice in my eyes and my tone. "No, I won't be needing more *water*." I absolutely refused to use his oh-so-quaint term, "skyjuice." It was the kind of thing an idiot considered clever. And they'd be wrong, just like they were wrong when they thought mullets ever looked cool.

"How about a plate of avocado toast?" He had that oh-so-servile expression on his admittedly handsome face. "We locally source the bread and the avocado is certified organic fair trade."

"I fully support your efforts to buy local and organic, but I'm going to have to pass, thank you," I smiled as politely as my ever-thinning patience allowed. I liked coming here, and I didn't want to be "that girl" who treated the wait staff like crap, but *God* I wished this guy would buzz off.

"Well, then what about a biscotti? We have a variety of flavors to choose from, chocolate, caramel, wheatgrass…"

"I'm fine, thank you." My tone was sharp, my patience nearly at an end. He finally took the hint and flitted off to speak with some chick with green hair and a nose ring.

I guess I found other ways to piss off my father than facial jewelry.

It wasn't often the heir to a gun manufacturing empire went pro-gun-control, after all.

Once Man Bun no longer irritated me with his presence, I used my cell phone to turn on the camera and check the feed. My hair had been pulled into a braid behind my head, so I looked more professional, and only light makeup adorned my face. I didn't have the confidence to go sans cosmetics entirely, not with how cruel the internet could be. I was a little bloated from my cycle during one of my podcasts and half the comments were about how I'd gotten "fat" since the previous week.

"Hello, and welcome to another edition of the *Common Sense Gun Laws* podcast. I'm your host, Scarlett Shaw."

Good, good, no flubs or mistakes. I hated having to go back and edit. Growing more confident, I continued my presentation.

My gaze narrowed, but I struggled to keep my anger out of my voice. Conviction was fine, but if you showed too much anger, the 'net would gripe about how you didn't have control of your emotions.

My father used to say there was no such thing as an unloaded gun and insisted we practice utmost safety. When I was a young girl, shooting was fun. It wasn't until I got older and became "woke" that I realized the truth.

My family were merchants of death, and it was up to me to try and do whatever I could to end that rule.

I banged my fist on the table for emphasis as I continued my podcast.

The podcast went on, with me ranting (intelligently) about the societal ills caused by reckless gun ownership. A lot of folks thought I shouldn't speak up about gun violence because it hurt the family business. Those folks could shut it.

After I wound down, I stopped the recording and checked the replay. I didn't need any editing other than making my teeth a little brighter. It'd been months since I had a treatment, and my coffee habit had taken its toll.

Mr. Man Bun came over to give me my check, and I made sure to tip him twenty percent. Even though he was annoying, he deserved to make a living like anyone else. As I gathered up my things and prepared to leave the café, I turned notifications back on and my cell phone blew up with messages.

A lot of it I didn't really care about. Why was Mindy bitching about Kevin? Of course, a man-ho like him was going to cheat on her with her cousin. And I was so over the drama between Kelly and Anna. Like, they need to hug it out or something for real.

But then I got to the good stuff. My best friend Lacey mass-texted the entire crew.

Rave tonight! A long profusion of emojis followed. Lace tended to overuse them. *Mason's dad's warehouse, 9 p.m. Wear a fairy tale themed outfit or you won't make it in the door.*

Jesus Christ, Lace, give the emoji button a rest.

The replies came in after, and it was important to go through them all and see what had been "claimed." Fairy tale theme meant that my go-to character, the Little Mermaid, would be a shoo-in. I make a good mermaid, and not just because of my red hair or penchant for wearing tiny outfits.

"Damn it," I cursed, gritting my teeth and glaring at Mindy's text saying she'd claimed the Little Mermaid for herself. "Fucking bitch."

I laughed at my own private put-down and kept scrolling. Jasmine was gone, so was Snow White. *Damn it, what's even left?*

Nothing good, that was for certain. I realized I was going to have to reach into the bag of actual fairy tales and not mass-produced family friendly animation for my costume.

Then I found it, the perfect character, and one that hadn't been tapped by multi-billion-dollar entertainment companies: Little Red Riding Hood.

"Yeah," I grinned at the screen. "I can work with this."

My fingers danced over the keys on my phone, sending missives out to my social circle. It turned out Lacey and Krista didn't have their outfits put together, either. It wasn't hard to convince them to join me on an excursion to my favorite boho boutique, *Scandals*. People can find a lot of gently used clothing there if they're willing to sift through row upon row of clothing racks.

We met up in the parking lot, Lacey in her own car while Krista and I relied upon Ryd. Lacey was almost six feet tall, a former college volleyball player and one of the loveliest blondes I'd ever seen. On that day she wore tight biker shorts and a tank top, but she'd always been good at presenting the athletic chic. Me, not so much. Krista's dad was from Puerto Rico, which was evidenced in her lovely brown skin, but not so much in her rigidly conservative viewpoints. I made a note then and there not to ruin our shopping trip by bringing up gun control because we didn't see eye to eye. *At all.*

Scandals was built into a narrow structure between two high-end jewelry stores, utterly packed to the brim with clothing racks to the point where we had to move single-file between them.

"Here, Scar." Lacey held up a red hooded half sweatshirt which left the belly daringly exposed. "This just screams Little Red Riding Hood."

"Oh, come on, Lace," Krista rolled her dark eyes. "Scar is too ma*chest*ic for that to fit."

"Machestic?" Lacey arched a brow. "Are you trying to say majestic?"

"No," Krista grinned, holding her hands out in front of her in the universal sign language for gigantic mammary glands. "Ma-*chest*-ic."

They enjoyed a laugh at my expense, which was fine with me since I saw being busty as a good problem to have.

With some help from my friends and the salesclerk, we cobbled together my costume—a red satin dress with a hugging bodice and a lace-up back, the skirt scandalously short. I knew it would flip up during my dance floor gyrations and reveal my panties, but that was the point. Thigh-high black stockings finished off the base of my outfit.

A short red hooded cloak, terminating about mid-back, and a ruffled pair of opaque panties finished the look. Adding a few light-up accessories and heavy lip gloss, I wound up appearing very much like what someone would order from an escort service if they were into Riding Hood kink. In other words, *just right* for a rave party.

Little did I know at the time that soon enough I would be running into a flesh and blood Big Bad Wolf who would change my entire world.

Chapter Three

Will

THE CRISP AUTUMN AIR STILL POSSESSED THE CLEAN smell of recent rain when I first shadowed Scarlett Shaw. I always loved the city after a good, hard rain. It significantly diminished the urine smell, even in the subways. But I refused to let the pleasant weather intrude on my professional duty.

When stalking prey, it's important to maintain a certain degree of detachment. This was exceedingly difficult when I had to get to know my target so intimately in order to carry out the objective. I'd known professionals in my line of work who'd assigned repellent nicknames to their targets to avoid growing any sort of attachment.

For me, it's a lot easier to do than for most. I had no illusions about the nobility of the male of the human species. Sorry, fellas, but face the facts. We started all the wars, we committed all the mass shootings, and I could count the number of female serial killers with the fingers of one hand. I'd need an entire Marine platoon sans shoes and socks to count male serial killers, and it still wouldn't be enough.

So, in my way of thinking, a man on this planet over the age of eighteen was guilty of something. Period, end of story, fuck you too. Especially if they were guilty of something and the Lone Wolf wound up on their trail.

But with women, it was a lot harder to remain detached. Taking into account the aforementioned poor character of men, they'd had to deal with us their entire lives. So even if they'd done illegal or immoral things, it was taken with a grain of salt.

That's why my usual rules were no women, no kids. But Devlin was right about my need to prove my loyalty to the family and the firm. *Mayhem Brothers, LLC's Prodigal Son Returns* was only a good headline so long as said prodigal son delivered when it counted.

So, there I was, breaking my own rules, and tracking a female target through Manhattan. A person might think a six-foot-two-inch, two-hundred-and-twenty-pound man would have a hard time blending into a crowd, and they'd be right. But I had many tools in my arsenal, the foremost of which was knowledge.

Anyone ever wonder why celebrities and criminals on the run tended to wear ball caps and sunglasses? Because it worked. The main things eyewitnesses remembered other than ethnicity and sex were hair and eye color. Wearing a baggy sweater, I blended pretty well with the general populace. If someone has never tried hiding in plain sight before, I suggest they do so. It works.

One of the old salts who trained me lamented the fact that newspapers have fallen out of vogue since they're so easy to hide behind. But trust me, if someone stares at their phone no one will look twice, unless it's to make sure the person is not about to run into them.

Thus, that day I waited outside the condo Hunter Shaw still covered for his darling daughter in the crisp autumn air, waiting for her to make an appearance. Other than a homeless man who asked me for change—I gave him a quarter, so as not to appear too generous and stick out in his mind—no one paid me the slightest attention as I sat at a sidewalk café nursing my coffee and waiting for my target.

In the meantime, I read up on her as much as possible. She was the eldest child of Hunter Shaw and definitely the black sheep of the family. Rather than attend Harvard like the rest of her siblings, she chose the more liberal leaning Brown. Graduated in the top five percent of her class, with a degree in Sociology. Smart girl. Liked hitting up those self-proclaimed "jazz clubs" where white college kids pretended they had the blues. Volunteered for the Human Hug Project.

Definitely not the immoral type who usually ended up on my radar.

I tried to console myself with the knowledge that she was going to be turned over to her father safe and sound when this was over. Still, I planned to do something terribly traumatic to her, and it seemed to me that being born rich shouldn't be enough of a crime to get the Lone Wolf breathing down your neck.

I detected movement out of the corner of my eye near her building entrance and snapped my gaze that way. When I saw that shock of red lustrous flowing mane, I knew it had to be my target.

Seeing her in person for the first time was quite the revelation. Wasp-waisted but curvy, Scarlett made no effort to hide her body from the masses. She had adorned herself in those miniscule, tight shorts that look sort of like 1980s high school gym gear only far sexier. They were a tempting green to match her eyes, with a white stripe down the side.

Her lovely legs, dusted with a cinnamon sprinkle of freckles, were bare. Strappy sandals adorned her feet, displaying her red-painted toenails. A little thin ankle chain glinted in the early fall sunlight as she chatted merrily with the ancient doorman.

The camisole she wore was a light yellow, complementing her ensemble, and her hair had been drawn into twin pigtails which trailed down her shoulders. Just about every man who wasn't completely distracted took a long, lingering look as she passed.

I tossed a twenty on the table, slammed down what was left of my coffee, and rose to my feet to tail her. On a pleasant day like today, the streets were crowded with pedestrians—tourists, shoppers, influencers, and street artists. Typical New York City mix. Fortunately, it made my task much easier.

Following Scarlett, I struggled to maintain my detachment. But damn, it was hard. Scarlett was nice to everyone, it seemed. When she bought a street pretzel from a heavyset Cuban woman, Scarlett paid with a fifty and didn't accept change. I'd seen people who got off from virtue signaling, but in her case I was pretty sure she honestly just wanted to help out of a sense of altruism.

Damn it, I thought. I didn't want to like this spoiled rich girl from the Upper East Side, a trust fund princess who had every advantage and every reason to turn into a total bitch. Except, she didn't. She cared about people. That was what stuck with me. She actually cared.

It reminded me of the deep sense of apathy I'd been battling ever since Devlin absconded with the girl I loved. I refused to say or even think of her name. Whereas I had grown bitter, Scarlett had grown warm.

She made it to Lincoln Square on foot, obviously without a care in the world. She didn't bother to check her corners or watch strangers to see if one of them might be a threat. While I realized this would make my job easier if she wasn't paying attention to her surroundings, I also cringed on the inside at the thought of how vulnerable she left herself.

A large crowd of protestors gave me the opportunity I needed. It seemed that one of the boutiques on the square had been selling fur from an endangered species of ermine. About fifty angry college kids and aging hippie PETA activists carrying signs and chanting slogans made it clear they had made a mistake.

As Scarlett tried to navigate through the milling throng, I moved around the crowd and "accidentally" bumped into her.

"I'm sorry," I mumbled with some sincerity, patting her on the shoulder to distract her from the fact I snatched her cell phone out of her purse. This was going to be the tricky part. I had to get somewhere private, jack open her case, and implant my little spying device, which would make me privy to all of her communications and data. And I had to do it before a social media addict such as her would check her phone again, which could happen at any moment.

I slid away through the crowd and checked over my shoulder at the edge. Scarlett wasn't looking at me at all. Instead she was chatting with one of the protestors. I guess they found some common ground.

Moving quickly, I ducked under a closed down falafel booth, the interior oddly lit from sunlight filtering through a white plastic tarp. Using my Swiss Army knife, I unscrewed the tiny bolts from the power jack and lifted the case open carefully.

The chip went into place and I closed the phone case. When I checked my success with my own cell, a grin spread over my features. It had worked like a charm. I now had access to all of her emails, chats, contacts, and —though I wouldn't be needing them—automatic logins for things like her credit cards.

Then came the tricky part. I came out of the falafel stand and saw that Scarlett still spoke with the protestor. All I had to do was get close enough to shove her phone back in her purse.

But as I worked my way through the crowd, Scarlett's brows rose as she made some sort of query. The protestor nodded and then she started digging into her purse, probably for the phone that was in my hand.

I cursed silently as she started to panic, digging more frantically in her purse for the device. There was no way I would be able to sneak the phone back in so long as she actively searched for it.

I improvised, kneeling down to tie my shoe while really sliding the phone across the ground to come to a rest between her sandals. Then I waited, and sure enough, she looked down at the ground. Relief spread over her freckled face, and she swiftly retrieved the device before taking a selfie with the protestor. Probably going to end up on her social media profiles.

Straightening, I left Scarlett to her own plans—and hacked device. There was no further need to follow her, as I'd seen all I needed.

When I filched her phone, I'd felt about in her purse enough to know she had no weapons in it other than pepper spray, which could be a pain in the ass but was hardly enough to stop someone like me. This combined with her penchant for traipsing about without a care in the world would make her easy prey for this big bad wolf.

However, I couldn't entirely ignore the guilt growing in my belly. As I said, most of my targets really had it coming, trust me. But in Scarlett's case, she truly seemed to be an innocent whose only crime was being born into the wrong family.

I wrestled with this for a time, but all I had to do to steel my resolve was remember my tenuous position in the firm. Devlin and my other brothers would be watching me very closely to make sure I had truly, fully committed to them and the family business.

It was meager balm for my soul, and I knew it wouldn't make things any easier for the poor girl I was about to snatch, but it was all I had.

Chapter Four

Scarlett

The pulsing throb of the high tempo electronic dance music vibrated through our bodies as we entered the loft. My mouth fell open in wonder at the dazzling laser lights and billowing smoke, which filled the senses, creating a chaotic landscape awash in swirling, scantily clad bodies.

"Wow, he spared no expense. Did he?"

"What?" Lacey squinted at me.

Leaning my hand on her bare shoulder, I put my mouth right next to her ear. "I said, he spared no expense. Did he?"

"Oh yeah, he always goes all out," Lacey grinned. Next to us, Krista talked the bouncer into taking a photo of the three of us in our rave costumes.

Lacey settled on Jasmine, dressed in diaphanous blue silk halter and blousy pants, which displayed her thong underwear beneath. I really thought Krista would make a better Jasmine, because of her complexion, but my other companion decided to be slutty Sleeping Beauty. Her pink dress featured a neckline so plunging she had to put tape over her nipples, and of course the skirt rode high enough to constantly display her matching panties because it was a rave and certain standards had to be upheld.

Me, I knew I looked cute, but seeing the three of us together at the same time in our outfits was Instagram-worthy. While we shared the pic between the three of us, I glanced around at the dance floor to see if I could spot anyone I knew.

It really was packed, the building threatening to burst at the seams. I spotted Mindy in her Little Mermaid outfit sashaying around in a hobble skirt, but other than that, I found that most of the attendees were strangers.

Krista and Lacey hooked up with this total dweeb named Joel who was the weird kid no one liked in high school but had turned into the number one X dealer for our social group. I didn't do X during high school—still don't—and since Joel was such a creep, I headed off on my own.

A song I really loved throbbed out over the speakers, masterfully mixed by a DJ wearing a light-up bull mask with anime features. I joined the swirl of molten gyrations, shaking everything I had and then some.

The great thing about the raves thrown by my peeps was that guys who got all creepy were shown the door in a hurry. So, when some guy got up a little too close, all I had to do was spin away from him and he would catch the hint and leave me alone, lest he be ejected. Fortunately, I didn't have to fend for myself for too long, as Lacey and Krista soon rejoined me.

We formed the Triad, so we could prevent any weird guys from dancing with us. I knew that a lot of guys got frustrated by this, but let me say we didn't owe anyone a dance, or access to our bodies for that matter.

At one point during our sweaty ritual Lacey leaned in and shouted in my ear. "Don't look now, Scar, but the Big Bad Wolf is totes checking you out."

Big Bad Wolf? I followed her gaze to the edge of the dance floor. Sure enough, a real brute of a man leaned up against a support pillar, watching me intently through the eyes of his stylized wolf mask that covered the top half of his face. My gaze ran over his bare upper torso, which was adorned only with a He-Man type of harness. His leather pants were about two seasons out of style, but he wore them well. *Quite* well.

I didn't know what his face looked like, but judging from his body, he kept himself in terrific shape. I put a little more swing in my hips as I danced, putting on a show for him. I even made sure to pirouette hard enough my skirt was sure to flip up and expose my ruffled panties.

Not saying I wanted to fuck the guy, not at all. I just liked the attention. But still my heart beat much faster when he suddenly broke away from the pillar and swept across the dance floor toward me.

He wasn't rude. He didn't push, but the crowd just kind of... parted for him. Like they could feel his presence coming and instinctively moved out of the way. I felt it too, smacking into me like a lead sheet. Those piercing, intense liquid blue eyes held me mesmerized, my body gyrating on instinct and rhythm rather than conscious thought.

Lacey and Krista spotted his approach. Lace gave me a wink and then the two of them swirled away to give me some private time with the Big Bad Wolf himself. Big muscle guys usually took themselves too seriously to dance, so my jaw dropped open when he pranced toward me like he was in a hip-hop video. His movements were graceful, like liquid, and I could tell right then he was a serious athlete. Maybe even a professional, given the upper crust patronage at the rave.

We started off dancing near each other, growing closer and closer as our gazes locked. Suddenly his hand snapped out and grabbed the small of my back, pulling me in tightly against him. I remember gasping at his audacity, but the thrill that ran through me drowned out any anger I may have experienced.

Besides, it felt really good to be pressed up to him like that, the hard bulge in his leather as distinct as it was exciting. We swayed together, moving to the beat and with each other. He swept me backward, dipping my head toward the floor while holding my lower back. I submitted to him, arching backward and going limp until he dragged me back up to my feet.

Our lips were so close, within inches of each other. I could smell his pleasant but not overpowering aftershave and the whiskey on his breath. For what seemed an eternity we remained like that, him devouring me with his gaze.

Then he leaned over and spoke into my ear in a rich, deep baritone more confident than God. "Come with me."

He didn't ask. He simply commanded. While I hated presumptuous, arrogant guys, this was different. Like he'd stated a fact, I was going to come with him and my choice in the matter was irrelevant.

I allowed him to tug me off the dance floor, his massive hand enveloping my own. He would occasionally cast a glance over his shoulder at me, those eyes behind the wolf mask as hungry as ever.

We moved right past the bar, which didn't bother me at the time because I was ready to go. My panties were damp already, and we hadn't even kissed. He led me up the floating staircase to the upper deck of the loft, which had been curtained off into different chambers. Ironically called the "quiet rooms," these places were ostensibly for people to chill out but everyone used them for make outs, and sometimes full-blown sex. The loud as hell music made perfect cover noise.

Indeed, two bodies were silhouetted through one of the curtains, making the beast with two backs. He paused before the curtain, staring intently at them before turning his gaze pointedly to me.

A shiver ran down my spine as he pulled me along behind him once more. His big hand parted a silver curtained chamber and we entered it together, seating ourselves on the comfy leather loveseat inside.

"I—I'm not normally like this." I was unable to meet his gaze now that we were alone.

"Not like what?" His gaze ran up and down my body, lingering on my breasts and thighs.

"Like this… you know, all… I mean, I don't even know your name."

"You know my name," he moved in and kissed me on my neck. My mouth flew open, hands instinctively going up to caress his hair and finger the strap of his mask. Did I know this guy? I thought I would have remembered someone with this build in my circle.

"Who—who are you?" I groaned as his hands pawed at my breasts through the laced-up bodice.

"I'm the Big Bad Wolf," he growled, suddenly crushing himself on top of me. He mashed his lips over my own, invading my mouth with his probing tongue and sucking my breath away. I responded in kind, my hands moving over his broad shoulders and fingering the ridges of muscle I found along the way.

Most of all, the Big Bad Wolf tasted delicious. I found that kissing him was as addictive as a drug, and he seemed to feel the same way about me. I'd dated before, even had a few guys I would have classified as boyfriends, but that was the most intense make out I think I ever had.

Wolf pinned me down on the loveseat beneath his massive bulk, spreading my thighs with his pelvis as he lay atop me. I moaned so loudly I could hear it over the heavy bass when his rock-hard cock rubbed against my panty-covered pussy. I think I even hooked my legs over the back of his knees, practically inviting him to ravish me.

His mouth moved down my neck, carefully kissed my cleavage, and went down farther still. Then I felt his fingers playing at the waistband of my ruffled panties, tugging them inexorably down.

Oh my God, this is really happening, I thought, without a touch of regret. I wanted him inside of me right that instant.

I moaned as he slid my panties down over my stockings and off completely. He wadded them up in his hand and then lay down on top of me once more.

"Protection?" I managed to gasp, desperately clasping my body against his.

"We won't be needing it," he growled. Before I could insist that *yes, we did need protection*, he suddenly stuffed my wadded-up panties into my mouth. Just like that, quick as a striking snake.

My eyes went wide, and a confused sound came from my gagged mouth, but I didn't panic. I just thought maybe that was his thing, making a girl taste her own arousal on her panties while he fucked her. Not my jam, but whatevs.

But then he grew rough, and not in a good way. He reared up and flipped me over onto my belly like I weighed nothing. The confused sounds escaping my mouth became angry grunts as he painfully yanked my arms behind my back. Something hard and cold and metal snapped around my wrists.

He had just handcuffed me. Still, some part of me thought it was surely a sex thing, and I didn't fight as hard as maybe I should have.

"I'm sorry, Scarlett," he murmured in my ear as he yanked the drawstring off my bodice, unveiling my breasts and even a peek of my pink nipples. "I really am sorry."

Now I panicked because he knew my name and I hadn't told him. Except, all my kicking and screaming behind the panties in my mouth were for naught. He was so strong, so explosive and fast, that he used my drawstring to tie the panties securely into my mouth.

He crossed and bound my ankles with his chest harness, and then lifted me bodily onto his shoulder. I made as much noise as I was able, but even I couldn't hear myself over the throbbing dance beats.

I kept thinking, *surely someone will notice this man carrying me away on his shoulder trussed up like a Thanksgiving turkey*. But no one paid us much heed. Even the bouncer laughed as Wolf carried me by. The worst thing of all was that my short skirt rode up and everyone could see my exposed bottom and nether lips. Not that it was all that shocking at a rave.

"Looks like Little Red Riding Hood got herself *caught*," the bouncer chuckled.

"You know bitches. This is totally her thing," the Wolf responded.

Despite my furious struggles, all the bouncer did was laugh even harder. Wolf carried me past the elevator and instead, took us to the fire stairs, his boots clomping loudly the whole way down. Here I was able to be heard, at least by him, and I gave him an earful.

"Settle down. Be a good girl and we'll get you back to Daddy as soon as he pays up."

That's when I realized that I was being kidnapped. And there wasn't a damn thing I could do.

Chapter Five

Will

Scarlett squirmed and whimpered on my shoulder, stabbing my heart with guilt with every nuanced noise. Not that I slowed my stride or considered setting her free for a moment as I made the forty-flight descent to street level.

She only weighed a little over a hundred pounds, but that was a long way to carry any sort of weight—hell, even no weight at all. I was glazed with sweat and huffing a little by the time we made it to the ground floor.

There, I found the large rolling suitcase I'd cleverly left in place. I could get away with carrying a tied-up girl over my shoulder at a wild rave party. That was not even the most shocking thing I saw in my brief visit. Carrying one through the streets of Manhattan when everyone had a cell phone on them, even the homeless guys, was not a prospect I wanted to entertain.

I set her down on the tiled floor and unzipped the case. Scarlett stared up at me, eyes swimming with conflicting emotions. While she was definitely afraid, there was also more than a little anger in her emerald gaze. Somehow she managed to look quite regal sitting trussed up on the floor, black drawstring holding ruffled panties in her mouth and tits on display.

She made a groan of alarm when I laid the open suitcase down next to her. Scarlett shook her head rapidly as I lifted her up and placed her inside.

"Settle down. No one's going to hurt you." I shoved her legs back inside the case when she tried to thrust them out. I wound up having to close the flap and lie on it so I could zip it closed because she wouldn't stop fighting.

Brave, but inconvenient. I could still detect her angry muffled protests through the suitcase, but they were much fainter than before. I doffed the wolf mask and put on my shirt, because I didn't want to draw attention.

I lifted the case carefully up onto its wheels and then tugged her along behind me. She squealed when I thumped her pretty hard across the metal door frame and out onto the street.

"Sorry, Red." I sincerely was apologetic. "I'll try not to jostle you too much, okay?"

My own voice sounded simpering to my ear. Since when did I try to curry favor with my target?

Shaking it off, I tugged her along outside the building and then cut through a darkened alley. A couple of urchins stopped talking as we passed, staring at me intently. All I had to do was reach down and pull up my shirt so they could see the handle of my pistol, and they quickly found something else more interesting in the alley.

I emerged from the alley next to a '76 Cordoba with a gold paint job. Not the most nondescript vehicle in the world, but it had a huge trunk, which was precisely what I needed.

After popping the trunk, I squatted down and bodily lifted the suitcase with the squirming, bound girl inside and placed it carefully into the vehicle. Then I slammed the trunk shut and moved to the driver's seat, resisting the impulse to look around and see if anyone watched. The last thing a person wanted to do in a situation like this was act like they were up to no good.

My heart hammered in my chest even as I pulled into traffic and headed toward the Jersey Turnpike. Until I got her to my safe house, I was in a lot of danger. Any number of things could have gone wrong. Her friends could have seen me carry her out and alerted the authorities, or maybe a security camera I had missed was taping over in the loft itself. I was pretty sure I got them all, though.

In any event, I rolled along with the traffic, listening to the radio and trying to act casual. A member of New York's Finest pulled up next to me in his cruiser, and I smiled at him. He frowned in response and patted his shoulder. What was he up to?

With a start, I realized I'd neglected to secure my seat belt. Pointedly, I made a surprised face and snipped it into place. The cop nodded, and even grinned a little as we pulled away from the red light.

The whole time we were on the street together, I kept expecting him to turn on his lights and come after me. Then I turned onto the Jersey pike and he continued going straight, and I heaved a sigh of relief. I "borrowed" this car, and if that cop had pulled me over, I had none of the essential paperwork to prove it was insured, or, you know, mine.

It was stop-and-go traffic through the Lincoln Tunnel, as usual, and I worried about Scarlett in the back. Would she have enough air? Of course, she would. I'd done this before, though never with someone as lovely as her. She would be fine, I knew, on a logical level, yet I couldn't stop thinking about her.

I couldn't stop thinking about us being on the dance floor together, either. Or the sensation of her body against mine as I took her lips in the quiet room at the rave. At the time I'd so wanted to fuck her. Badly. Part of me even tried to rationalize it as part of the scheme, but logically I knew better.

It just wouldn't have been right to take her pussy when I was already planning her abduction.

Damn but I wanted to, though.

Even when she was on my shoulder, I'd been keenly aware of how scantily clad she really was. No panties were there to keep my eyes or my touches away…

That's not how I rolled, though. The Lone Wolf didn't rape women. He didn't need to. Their panties dropped whenever he wanted. Or so I told myself while trying to deny the rock-hard erection I endured all the way across the river to New Jersey.

There's a lot of stereotypes about Jersey, and to be fair, a lot of sophisticated and intelligent people live there. However, there are also enough big-haired, loud-mouthed, ignorant fashion disasters to make the stereotypes endure over time.

It's not my favorite place in the world, but the rent is about a third what I'd pay in New York City. The firm is a profitable one partially because we run it like a business, including cutting costs. I probably could have rented a safe house in the city and put it on Devlin's tab, but I was trying to get back into the good graces of the family, so I played it by the book, so to speak.

At any rate, my safe house was on the outskirts of Jersey, barely within the city limits. There's a strip of beach close to a water treatment plant, and the smell keeps it undeveloped for the most part. My safe house appeared as a run-down formerly glorious home right on the beach, though most of the windows were boarded over. The second floor was mostly uninhabitable save one of the bedrooms because of all the junk piled around, but the first story was spacious and comfortable.

I parked the Cordoba in the garage in the back and then popped the trunk. At first, the stillness and quiet made me fear Scarlett had in fact died during our drive. Maybe she choked on her panties? Or suffocated due to lack of air?

But as soon as I grabbed the zipper and tugged, she got to squealing again. The zipper flashed down, splitting the canvas and revealing her angry freckled face. She carefully articulated as best she could around the panties in her mouth.

"Yoo sug ug uh biff."

"Yeah, I know," I sighed. "Trust me. I don't like this any more than you do, all right? You have every right to be pissed off."

I lifted her out of the case directly and sat her bare butt on the bumper. She glared at me as I unstrapped her legs so she could walk. Then I grabbed her arm and dragged her to her feet.

"Let's go." I kept my tone low, tugging her along to stumble beside me through the garage. Her green eyes flashed all over the place, probably trying to get an idea of where we were. I should have blindfolded her, but it wasn't like she really knew our location.

I helped her up the short flight of stairs into the house proper and then shoved her ahead of me through the clean and tidy kitchen and into the living room. There would be a gorgeous view of the ocean here, if not for the boarded-up windows.

My palm rested on her cheek, and I glared right into her eyes.

"Stay put." Then I patted her face gently to take some of the sting out of my harsh words. She watched, fearful but silent, as I dragged a stout chain from where it rested in a coil next to the wall. I'd secured a long bolt into the stud earlier and added a padlock to the end.

The free end encircled her left ankle, and then I padlocked that as well. It was snug, but had enough clearance she wouldn't lose circulation.

She made a strangled sob when I roughly turned her face away from me, her skirt riding up so I could see her naked ass.

"Relax," I said. "If I wanted that, I'd have taken it at the rave when you were begging for my cock."

Scarlett made an angry noise and squirmed, which made me angry as I dropped the keys to her cuffs several times. Finally, I'd had enough. I snaked my arm around her torso and clamped my hand firmly around her snow-white throat.

"Settle. The fuck. Down." I growled in her ear, squeezing just tightly enough to show I could easily snap her neck. Scarlett froze, though she still shivered in fear. I bent myself to the task of removing her cuffs and this time succeeded.

Then I went to work on the drawstring knotted around her head while she rubbed her wrists. I picked out the knot and pulled the string away. She quickly reached up and removed the sodden panties from her mouth.

I turned her around to face me, intent upon laying down the ground rules of our babysitting arrangement. A flash of anger sparked in her green eyes, and I saw the slap coming a mile away, but I didn't stop her. I stood there and let her hit me. I figured she deserved that much satisfaction, at least.

And let me tell you, she put some stank on it. The resounding slap echoed through the largely empty house and left my cheek stinging.

"You fucking bastard," she snarled. "I could have died in that suitcase. I don't know who you think you are, but…"

My hand clamped over her mouth, and I backed her into a nearby chair until she sat. I glared at her for a long moment, so she knew without a shadow of a doubt who was in charge, and then removed my palm, now stained with her lipstick.

"Yes, I'm a fucking bastard. You have every right to hate me. But we're going to be spending a few days together, so let's lay down some ground rules. One: No screaming. Two: No hitting. Three: You will do what I say, when I say. Follow those rules, and you won't be hurt."

"What do you want?" She licked her lips. I swallowed hard because she was so damn smoking hot in that little trollop outfit, the pink tips of her nipples peeking through and her skirt ridden up scandalously high.

"Money, of course. The people I represent will be sending your father a ransom note soon. Speaking of which…."

I picked up an old-style Polaroid camera and snapped her picture. She blinked against the flash, and then the resulting photo machined its way out. I shook the photo as she laughed.

"What's so funny?" I asked, growing angry. I wasn't used to being mocked in this type of situation when I clearly had all the power.

"You are, idiot," she answered hotly. "If you knew the first thing about me, you'd know my dad would never waste money trying to get me *back*. He hates my guts."

Well, fuck. There was a complication if I ever heard one.

Chapter Six

Scarlett

THE BIG BAD *BASTARD'S* FROWN DEEPENED, AND FEAR tightened in my gut. As if I could be more freaked out!

Breathe, I reminded myself. *Do your best not to lose your shit.*

If there was ever a time for me to lose my shit, this would be the time. Unfortunately, my inner voice had a point. I managed to throw the Big Bad Wolf for a loop. As long as I kept him jumping, he'd be too busy trying to score his payday to fuck with me. Perhaps, literally.

I shuddered at the thought.

The worst part? I still wanted to bang him. He pulled a bait and switch back at the party. Despite the fact that I was in obvious danger, the most animalistic part of my brain still ached for him. That part of my brain was a dumbass.

"You're lying." The Big Bad Wolf's frown morphed into a smirk. "Good try. You had me worried for a moment."

"I'm not lying. He can't stand me. I'm all but disowned. I had to sit at the kids' table last Thanksgiving." I probably shouldn't have shared that, but I overshared when I was nervous. My podcasts would be three-hour rants if I didn't take time to research and make detailed notes.

"He's still your father." Though the words were addressed to me, I got the feeling the Big Bad Wolf was trying to reassure himself. "He'll pay for your life."

"Maybe," I shrugged. "Or maybe he'll be glad I vanished."

The Big Bad Wolf tipped his head to one side. The idiotic part of me that still thought he was hot shivered. My eyes darted to his mouth as he tapped the tip of his tongue against his top lip. While the idiot part of my brain thought about what his mouth could do, the rest of me fantasized about punching out his teeth.

Would I be able to? I was a pacifist on principle, but I figured if there was ever a time to use a free pass, it was now. Physically, though, I wasn't sure if I could punch this guy. His chiseled jaw looked like it would break my hand if I tried.

"Why would he be glad?" the Big Bad Wolf murmured.

"I can't tell if you're joking or not."

He knelt down in front of me so he could look me in the eyes. I went rigid, ready to lash out or pull away if needed. There wasn't anywhere for me to go, but that didn't mean I wasn't going to fight him with all of my might.

"Why the fuck would I be joking?" His voice was a deep growl. Big Bad Wolf indeed.

"Seriously?" I did my best to sound nonchalant. I'd known guys like this before. They got off on control and dominance. Withholding that from him could either be really smart or insanely stupid. All I knew was my pride couldn't cope with cowering. If he wanted to have a go at me, I wouldn't make it easy for him.

"You're his oldest daughter, his firstborn. His baby girl." The Big Bad Wolf looked like he was going to trace a finger along my cheek but thought better of the action. Good. I would've bitten right through that fucking finger.

"You know enough about me to know that I'm the oldest, yet you don't know anything else?" I tipped my head, just as he had done earlier. I held eye contact. I needed him to know I was mocking him.

When he didn't answer, I took that as a sign to keep going.

"You must know what my father does for a living. Right? Or did you overhear someone say how rich he is and decide to kidnap me based on his checkbook?" I clicked my tongue and rolled my eyes. "Amateur."

"You're not in a position to be mouthing off," he snapped.

For a moment, I thought he might strike me. He certainly looked pissed enough to do it. I clenched my jaw, waiting for the hit, but it didn't come. Maybe he *was* telling the truth when he said he wasn't going to hurt me.

Except, getting put in a suitcase really fucking hurt.

"I'm just trying to make your job easier," I shrugged. "After all, the sooner your job is done the sooner I never have to set eyes on you again. Right?"

"That's the plan. Your father will pay."

"If I were you, I'd come up with a plan B," I said. "He's not going to pay."

"Why not? Did you sleep with the help or something?"

I rolled my eyes and scoffed. I tried not to look the Big Bad Wolf in the eye for more than a few seconds at a time. I had no idea what to make of him. Most of me was afraid, very afraid. Yet, I hadn't reached a point of blind terror. I knew I couldn't trust anything that came out of his pretty mouth, yet I also knew he spoke the truth when he said he wouldn't hurt me.

I wasn't about to start singing his praises just yet. The bar for men was pretty damn low, but not so low that I would forgive him literally fucking kidnapping me.

This guy was a Bad Guy, but he might not be a bad guy. At least, that was the only way my adrenaline-filled, tipsy brain could rationalize everything. If the rationalizing stopped, I'd go into a full-blown panic. That wouldn't get me out of here any quicker.

"Many times," I smirked. "But that's not why my father hates me."

"Hate?" He laughed dryly. "That's a strong claim."

"It's true. You know who my father is. Right?"

"Hunter Shaw," he recited. "The biggest and best gun manufacturer in the country."

"Right," I nodded. "And I'm his bleeding heart, pro-gun-control, liberal daughter. A *disgrace*."

"No way," he scoffed. "How can you come from a family like that and—"

"Have my own thoughts, opinions, and worldviews?" I cut in.

He looked me over for a moment before nodding. "Well, yes, actually."

"It wasn't easy," I said. "Many family dinners ended early because the arguing wouldn't stop. For all the differences between my father and me, we share one important trait."

"Stubbornness, no doubt," he sighed, effectively taking the wind out of my sails.

"Yes, actually." I looked away once more. "That's how I know he won't pay."

"You're still his flesh and blood." His voice softened. Not by much. Most people wouldn't have noticed the subtle change. Thanks to my unique upbringing, I recognized those minute changes more than most. Before I was smart enough to have my own ideas, my father had me sit in on deals. I couldn't sit at the table, of course. I had to sit at a small desk in the corner while the men talked about weapons and money.

"I think you're underestimating the love a father has for his daughter," the Big Bad Wolf said. Oddly sentimental for someone who'd stuffed my panties in my mouth and now held me for ransom.

"I think you're underestimating my father's love for his money," I replied. "I've cost him millions."

This surprised my captor. His brows shot up before he could regain his composure. "Millions? You're exaggerating."

"I have a podcast," I said, realizing too late that it sounded pretty lame considering the circumstances. "On more than one occasion, I've outlined exactly how my father has profited from the loose gun control laws in this country, despite the lives lost."

"You've got to be kidding," the Big Bad Wolf smirked. "Explain to me how a *podcast,*" he spoke through his laughter, "cost the Shaw Rifle empire *millions.*"

"New screening regulations were put forth," I said. "My father didn't comply. I leaked the proof. He had to sift through lawsuit after lawsuit for two years before it all went away."

"Shit." The Big Bad Wolf drawled and sat back on his heels. "Must be one hell of a podcast."

"Do you believe me now?" I asked. "He's not going to pay. If anything, he might pay you to send me away somewhere."

That could be a win-win. I didn't really want to relocate but… desperate times and all that. I could live in Brooklyn if it was *absolutely* necessary. Or maybe France? I could be happy in France. Bread and wine were all a girl needed, right?

"You're not joking. Are you?" He fixed me with an unshakable, calculating stare. Once again, I couldn't look into his eyes for more than a few moments. I hated breaking eye contact. It felt like I was somehow… submitting. Like hell would I ever submit to the likes of him.

Except you almost did, a little voice whispered in my mind. *You were practically begging for it.*

My cheeks grew hot.

"Yeah, I'm joking," I scoffed. "I decided that right now when I'm chained up like an animal, half-naked, with a strange man would be the perfect time to work on my stand-up routine."

To my surprise, he laughed.

"You're a funny one," he said. "I'll give you that. Losing millions of your father's *billions* isn't enough for him to sell your life away. He'll pay."

"Leaking his information wasn't my only accomplishment," I said. "I've led protests during his press conferences. I've vandalized his cars. Once, I tried to set fire to one of his assembly warehouses."

"No shit." It might have been the adrenaline, but I swore he looked impressed.

"Well, I lit a match and tossed it in the dumpster behind the building," I amended. "No one was hurt. Nothing was even damaged. He was still pissed though."

"I don't think that's enough for him to abandon you."

His words send a shiver down my spine.

"You've clearly never been the wayward child," I said. "You don't know what it's like to be the black sheep."

"That's where you're wrong." He sat down fully, about five feet away from me. He couldn't reach me if I were to try something. Then again, I couldn't reach him, either. We were both as safe as we were going to be, though he definitely had the upper hand. I was chained up for fuck's sake. What could I do?

Physically, nothing.

"What?" I frowned.

"I enlisted in the Army," he explained. "That's a big no-no in my family."

"Not a patriotic bunch?"

"I wouldn't say that," he said. "We view the law as a set of guidelines more than actual *rules*. That tends to piss off the people who make and enforce said rules. They're just mad we beat their system."

"Is that truly how you see it?"

"I know you may not believe me, but I have my own rules that I abide by. I don't agree to do jobs that violate that code." A strange look came across his face, just for a split second, before disappearing altogether.

"What a hero you are," I muttered.

"I never said I was a hero. I don't pretend to be," he snapped.

"That's for damn sure. Heroes usually do the rescuing, not the capturing." When he didn't say anything, I decided to press a little harder. Probably not the smartest idea, but if I could find a weak point to exploit, maybe I could get out of here faster. "Is this to get back in daddy's good graces?"

"I don't care if I'm in his good graces or not," he said with a dark look in his eye.

"Then why do this? You're not giving this your all."

"Are you criticizing my kidnapping methods?" He moved forward until his face was mere inches from mine. He moved so quickly I didn't have time to prepare myself. I pushed back into the wall as far as I could go, and I damned myself for not holding it together better.

The Big Bad Wolf knew he had the upper hand, but I didn't want him to know how much. Another unexpected lesson from my father reared its ugly head.

Never show your hand.

"I can make this far worse for you, little heiress."

"I'm *not* an heiress," I snapped.

"So, you paid for your clothing, your phone, your drinks at the club, and everything else on your own? Do you pay your rent? What about your car payments? Aside from your podcast, do you work?"

I clamped my mouth shut, seething with anger.

"That's what I thought, little heiress." He backed up until he was sitting once more.

"I'd rather you call me Red Riding Hood," I mumbled. "Besides, you know my name."

"I do," he nodded. "It's Scarlett Shaw."

"Do I get to know yours?"

He looked at me for a long time before speaking. "No."

"That's hardly fair," I pouted. "If I guess correctly, will you tell me?"

"What would you guess?" Humor danced in his eyes. If he wasn't so hell-bent on playing his part, he might've smiled.

"Stavros or something," I shrugged. "All the bad guys from the movies have names like that."

"This isn't a movie, Little Red." He got to his feet and turned his back to me. "Neither of us are that lucky."

Chapter Seven

Will

"I'm hungry," Scarlett lifted her gaze from her lap to meet my stare. "And cold. This outfit wasn't designed to be practical."

I glanced over at her from the boarded-up window and frowned. I'd been peering out through the cracks between the boards at a pair of senior citizens enjoying a stroll down the beach. This didn't sit well with me, as the seclusion of my safe house was its main selling point. It seemed complaints from the locals caused the water treatment plan to change its hours of operation.

Now the foul smells were mostly prevalent at night, meaning the beach wasn't the unpleasant place it once was during the daylight. I knew I'd have to be very intent upon security, particularly if I ever needed to leave the safe house.

Scarlett would not enjoy the process one bit. Normally I didn't care, but despite my best efforts, she grew on me. And it went far beyond a physical attraction. We had some common ground between us, both being the black sheep of our family lines. So, if I could avoid making her suffer, I would.

At the time, I wasn't worried. The safe house was to have been fully stocked with groceries and sundry items, as well as a change of clothes for my "guest." I shrugged and moved into the kitchen.

"I'll make dinner," I said, walking past her.

"If you unchain me, I can help," she called hopefully.

"Not going to happen," I snarled, though my tone seemed far less harsh than I'd intended. I think I knew then that she was really getting under my skin but didn't want to admit the truth.

I threw open the first cabinet door, and found it empty of everything but dust. Shrugging, I moved on to the next. And the next. Every time, with growing frustration, I found nothing but cobwebs met my efforts.

"What the fuck, Devlin?" I muttered and then grimaced. I had just dropped my brother's real name in front of Scarlett. Hopefully she didn't hear me.

"Who's Devlin?" she called from the living space, and I cringed. Some professional.

"Nobody," I said, shaking my head. "A ghost. I'm sorry, but it looks like I'll have to go out for food."

I could see her emerald eyes narrow and grow calculating. She was thinking her chances of escape shot through the roof if I wasn't present. Proving her wrong was not going to be a happy task.

"I see. What about something to wear?"

I looked over at her, still wearing the skimpy Red Riding Hood costume, sans underwear and with her bodice drawstring missing so she nearly flashed her tits every time she moved. No wonder she was cold and forced to cover herself with her arms.

"Probably not," I said with more regret than I thought I would. "But I'll pick you up some clothing, too."

"Do you need my measurements?" she asked helpfully. I arched an eyebrow at her.

"No need." I'd already gotten all of her info when I hacked her phone.

"I see," she swallowed hard. Her gaze couldn't quite meet my own.

"What's your problem?" I tried to sound tough, but it came out more like a soft request.

"I—I'm afraid to say it out loud," she said with a shiver.

"You've already been kidnapped, Scarlett," I shrugged. "Your situation can't get much worse."

"I can think of several ways it could be worse." She laughed and then her eyes sparkled. "I can think of several ways it could be better, too."

Her gaze flashed to my crotch for a split second. I didn't know if it was subliminal or a calculated manipulation. In either event, it worked because I pitched a tent right there and lost my train of thought. But then she spoke again.

"Look, I've seen enough shows and movies to know how this works." Her voice wavered and tears glistened in the corners of her eyes. "I've seen your face, so that means there's no way I'm walking out of this mess alive. Right?"

She sobbed, and I moved quickly over and kneeled in front of her chair, resting my hand on her bare knee.

"Hey, cut that out," my voice more pleading than insistent to my own ears. "You're going home in one piece."

"But I can…" she sniffled. "But I can identify you… you can't afford to let me go. I know how it works."

"Do you?" I asked. "Let me lay this on you, Scarlett. Did you know that less than ten percent of robbery suspects —unmasked, caught on *multiple* security cameras—get caught?"

"No," she said hopefully. "That doesn't sound right, though. I mean, if they were on camera…"

"Yeah, but surely you've lived long enough to have seen a person who reminded you of someone else? Maybe a lot like someone else. The truth is, eyewitnesses and even photographic evidence can't garner a conviction on their own. What are you going to tell the police? That some white guy with black hair took you captive? There's four million mooks just like me in New York City alone."

She laughed but still seemed unconvinced.

"I'm afraid you kind of stick out in a crowd, Wolf," she said. "For one thing, most guys aren't drop dead gorgeous in New York. Not even close."

There she went again. Trying to manipulate me. Still, I wound up smiling in spite of myself.

"That may or may not be true, but still… there are a dozen people who will swear to God and everyone that I was on a fishing trip upstate over this weekend. Prominent people, with connections. If the cops want to check, they'll even find that my cell phone data backs up this alibi. I'm a professional, Scarlett. I've babysat a ton of clients before you, and guess what? They all went home alive."

"Thank you," she wiped her tears. "I don't know if you're being honest with me or not, but I think you are, and it does help me feel better."

I nodded, but then heaved a heavy sigh.

"What's wrong?" she asked.

"I'm going to have to leave and collect some supplies," I said. "And that means I have to make sure you won't get up to any mischief while I'm gone."

Her eyes went wide, and she paled by several shades. After a shaky laugh, she lifted her chained ankle for my inspection.

"Come on, Wolf," she said in a pleading tone. "What am I going to do? Snap my chain and then pull a Princess Leia and choke you with it when you come home?"

I didn't change my expression or offer a comment.

"I'm sorry, for what it's worth." I headed out to the garage. I recovered some items from the trunk that I'd packed without ever intending to use them. Truly, I never thought I would leave her alone once we got to my safe house, but now I supposed it was a good thing I brought them.

Of course, I wished at the time that I'd had less foresight. I could have used that as an excuse to just trust the chain to keep her out of trouble. But my conscience wouldn't let me not use what I'd brought with me. I had to think about more than just me, or Scarlett for that matter. I had to consider my family, and the firm, and the fact that if she escaped, she would ironically be in more danger.

Scarlett whimpered when she saw what I brought in.

"No," she said. "Please. I'll just sit right here in this chair until you get back. I promise."

"I'm sorry, Scarlett," I whispered, handing her a pair of foam sponge balls. "Squeeze them tight, make a fist."

One thing about a babysitting gig is this: it's really, really, really hard to restrain someone in a way that they won't eventually be able to get out of. That crap you see in the movies doesn't fly. In order to ensure your guest remains out of trouble, you have to make them pretty uncomfortable.

She did as I told her, squeezing the foam balls. Then I slipped a pair of my—clean—calf-high sweat socks over her hands up to her elbows.

Scarlett's eyes welled with silent tears, but she made no more protests as I used a fuck ton of rope to lasso up her sock-shrouded arms. This took her fingers out of the equation.

I really didn't want to use the handcuffs, because they could damage the radial nerve during a struggle. And I knew she would be struggling as soon as I walked out the door and left her alone. Instead, I pulled her arms behind her back behind the chair and securely bound her wrists together with some rope.

Scarlett heaved an exasperated sigh as I wound tape around her waist and above and below her breasts.

"Jesus Christ, man, will you give it a rest? I'm obviously not going anywhere."

"I'll see to that," I muttered, though I'll admit I was probably going a bit overboard. I really didn't want her to get hurt, though, more so than I was worried about being caught.

Pro tip: you don't want to ever put duct tape on bare skin, unless you don't mind losing said skin. And I was determined that if I had any say in the matter at all, not one hair on her head would be harmed.

"Open your mouth," I said, holding up the device that made her whimper the most, a plastic ball gag with holes. No chance of it slipping down her throat and choking her, and the holes made it easy to breathe.

"No," she shook her head. "Please, I'll be quiet, I swear…"

"Open." More insistent that time. Then I added, as banal as it sounded, "For your own good, open up, Scarlett."

Sniffling, she closed her eyes and did what she was told. I shoved the ball into her mouth and pulled it deep behind her teeth. She groaned in protest, but if you didn't make these things really tight, the wearer could push them out with ease. Once it was buckled behind her head, I stepped away and felt a terrible stab of guilt looking at her trussed-up form.

"I'm sorry." It sounded lame to my own ears and I kissed the top of her head. "I'll be back soon, okay?"

Then I turned away and left quickly on legs rubbery with fading resolve. I went to the side of the room, dug out my phone and called my big brother Devlin.

"How's the gig going?" Devlin asked by way of answering his phone.

"How you think it's going, you son of a bitch?" I snapped.

"What's wrong? Did the client get away?"

"The client is secure." A stab of guilt hit me right in the heart. "But I'm heading on a grocery store run because some asshole forgot to stock up the beach house."

"Oh yeah, I did say I'd take care of that," Devlin laughed. "Sorry."

Fucker didn't sound sorry.

"Sorry? I'll show you sorry, pencil neck," I sputtered. "After this job is done, me and you are going to have words."

"Like the last time we had words, right before you left? Dental work is expensive, you know."

He was referring to my knocking out his front teeth after he stole my girlfriend, not threatening me with a beating. But I took the hint anyway. Family did not fight family. It's the first cardinal rule of the firm.

"Never mind," I muttered. "There might be another problem. Turns out the baby girl is estranged from dear old daddy. He might not cough up."

"He'll cough," Devlin assured me. "But if he doesn't… well, you understand the firm's reputation has to be… protected." I grew silent, and his tone was harsh when he spoke again. "Do you *understand*, Will?"

"Yeah. I understand," I snapped, ending the call.

If Scarlett's father didn't pay, Devlin had ordered me to kill her.

Chapter Eight

Scarlett

I tried not to look like I was eavesdropping. Technically, I wasn't. This place wasn't very big, from what I could tell. I heard his end of the conversation from where he stood. Aside from static mutterings through what I assumed was a burner phone, I couldn't make out what the person on the other end of the line was saying.

I'm sure the Big Bad Wolf got new instructions from some Bigger *Badder* Wolf.

"Stay here." My Wolf tugged on a jacket.

You're kidding, right? I wanted to say as much, but the ball gag made it impossible. Instead, I made a show of rattling my chains.

"Right," he chuckled. "Good point. I'm not worried. Any food allergies I should know about?"

I fixed him with the coldest stare I could muster. What was he? My fucking flight attendant?

"I'll avoid peanuts just to be safe. That's one of the most common ones. If you're allergic to processed wheat or something... well, you're shit out of luck." He reached for the door and then hesitated. "You're not one of those all-organic, free-range, fair-trade vegans, are ya?"

Again, I could only narrow my eyes.

"If you are, I'm not sure I can accommodate that," he continued. "We'll be lucky if I can get to anything more substantial than a 7-Eleven. I hope you like Cheeto puffs and powdered doughnuts. That might be all you get until tomorrow. I assume beer is fine?"

I let out an indignant squawk which only made him smile more.

Bastard. This isn't supposed to be fun for either of us.

"Do me a favor, will ya?" he asked. "Don't scream or anything. This will go better for everyone involved if you follow the rules like a good girl."

Oh, I'm definitely going to knock at least one of his teeth out before I'm rescued. That's a goddamned promise.

"You look like you're thinking very hard." He tilted his head. "Don't wear yourself out."

I rolled my eyes. He was lucky I had a gag in my mouth.

He hesitated by the door. Maybe he was trying to decide if leaving me unattended really was a smart idea. He didn't look back. Instead, he sighed and headed out.

Weirdly enough, now that I was alone, the realities of my situation felt far more terrifying. According to every crime show ever, this was the time I should have felt braver.

My wrists ached from my bindings. Getting free would be the first step to getting out of here. There might not have been much I could do about the handcuffs, but I could work with ropes.

I didn't notice it before, but I was quite familiar with the sort of knot my Big Bad Wolf has used to tie me up. Looked like I wasn't the only one with a little experience in this area. Shame he didn't take me up on my offer. I believed we could have a *ton* of fun in bed.

Thanks to a childhood of ballet and gymnastics, combined with yoga classes a few times a week, I was a spry little lady. It hurt like hell, but after twenty minutes of bending and twisting, I was able to get myself into a position where I could bite at my bindings.

Except, I'd forgotten one small detail. The fucking ball gag. That should have been a tip-off that the Big Bad Wolf was into some big bad things in bed.

Without free use of my hands, getting the ball gag off was going to be a unique challenge. I bent forward and turned my head as far to the side as it could go. Lifting my leg so that the side of my knee pressed against the gag fastening, I started moving my head. All I needed to do was loosen the restraint *just* enough to slip the gag down over my jaw.

I felt completely ridiculous, but I was now glad for my costume. My legs were mostly unrestricted, allowing that kind of movement to be possible. The fastening gave a tiny amount.

"Yef!" I cheered through the gag. A few more wriggles and the fastening was loose enough to slide down.

I stretched my jaw and rubbed my lips together. As far as ball gags went, that one wasn't the worst I'd ever experienced. They weren't my cup of tea in the first place, though, so what did I know?

The ropes would be another challenge. The Big Bad Wolf was pretty damn good at knots. If I didn't know which bit to tug on, I'd certainly be stuck here forever.

I took the bindings between my teeth and thrashed my head. It hurt. My jaw was still tender from being held open in such an odd way. I considered tearing through the rope with my teeth like some kind of goddamned woodland creature, but I didn't think I had enough bite power to pull it off.

Then again, some say we have the bite power to take a finger off as if it were a carrot. I didn't want to be the one to test that theory. Years of expensive retainers, braces, and other hardware made my pearly whites a well-earned prize.

Finally, the binding gave a little. More tugging, biting, and some uncomfortable tonguing ensued until the bindings went slack. Arms free, I tore the ball gag off completely.

"For fuck's sake," I muttered.

Once on my feet, I tried to take a look around the place. There must have been some kind of clue as to where I was. We drove for some time, but it felt like we sat in traffic for part of the journey. Either that or the Wolf delighted in stopping and going in rapid succession just to fuck with me. That seemed like a distinct possibility.

I took a step toward the kitchen when my leg was nearly yanked out from under me.

Right.

The fucking ankle chain. Even worse, I had to pee. The bathroom was too far away.

There had to be something nearby I could use to pick the lock. Unfortunately, the Wolf must have thought of that. There was nothing remotely useful within reach of me. I couldn't get to the kitchen—just the edge of the kitchen island. All of those sharp, pretty knives and tools weren't an option.

There was a coffee table pushed into the hallway with a few small drawers. I got on my hands and knees, crawled as far as I could, and reached for the closest drawer. It was empty.

"Bastard," I shrieked. "Fuck you, you stupid Big Bad Wolf Bastard! Fuck you! Fuck you! *Fuck! You!*"

I felt ten times better after that little outburst. It was quite cathartic. With a little luck, maybe someone heard me. With no other option, I continued to scream.

"Can anyone hear me?" I screamed as loudly as I could. My throat burned and ached, but I kept trying. It occurred to me that if anyone could hear me, they likely couldn't communicate that to me. Or maybe they were trying their best, but I couldn't hear them over my own screams.

I fell silent and waited for a few moments. When nothing happened, I began shouting once more.

"Can anyone help me?" I couldn't keep screaming like this. My throat was going to give out. If the Big Bad Wolf heard me, he might go back on his word about hurting me.

Dejected and out of ideas, I shuffled back to my chair. I wasn't about to put the bindings and ball gag back in place, but I figured I might as well get comfortable while I waited.

Twenty minutes later, the door unlocked, and the Big Bad Wolf stepped inside.

"Good news," he said. "I found an actual grocery store. Neither of us will have to eat like shit while we wait for your father."

"You're still convinced you're going to get your money?" I asked.

"Yes, I—hey, what the fuck?" He set the grocery bags down on the table before whirling around to look at me. His mouth dropped open in shock, but he quickly recovered. "Remind me to tighten the ropes next time. I was trying to be a gentleman and not cut off your circulation."

As much as he tried to resist, his eyes raked over my body. My bare legs were slightly parted, just enough to put myself on display. I felt what I felt when we were making out in the club. He wanted me. I just had to push him to the point where he could no longer resist me. It wasn't my favorite way to get the upper hand over a guy, but it was effective.

Besides, he looked like he'd be amazing in bed.

A lazy smirk spread across his mouth. "Nice try. That's not going to work."

"Are you sure?" I licked my lips.

"Positive." He returned his attention to the groceries. I couldn't help but notice the growing bulge in his pants.

"You didn't happen to get a change of clothes for me, did you?"

"Maybe I did," he shrugged. "Maybe I didn't."

"Bastard."

"That kind of talk isn't going to get you new clothes anytime soon," he tutted. "How did you get out of your bindings?"

"You don't tie knots as well as you think you do," I snapped. Now that the adrenaline had seeped out of my body, the cold set in. Goosebumps rose over every inch of my exposed skin. My teeth wanted to chatter, but I wouldn't let that happen.

"I know for a fact that's not true," he smirked. "You must be flexible. Yoga?"

"I—yes, actually," I muttered. "Good guess."

"Not a guess," he shrugged. "What about the ball gag? How'd you manage that?"

"I'm not going to tell you." I kept my eyes trained on him as he moved through the house, stocking the fridge and cupboards. Anxiety twisted in my stomach. Any moment now he'd snap and punish me for being disobedient. He must not have known I screamed for help. Fat lot of good that did me anyway. No one came running to my rescue.

Even if someone *did* come to my rescue, who could say whether or not they'd help me or take advantage?

God, I was so screwed.

"You look like you're about to panic." he called out to me.

"Is that so hard to imagine?" My heart threw itself against my ribcage. "I'm sure you're some kind of sociopath but can you at least *imagine* what this must be like from my point of view?"

"Did anyone ever tell you it's not wise to threaten your captor?" he shot back. "I'm not a sociopath, by the way. If I had a choice, I'd do this differently."

"Yes, they did. However, I've never been known to stick to a script," I said pointedly.

"You're joking, right?"

"I'm the daughter of one of the wealthiest men in the country. My father has literally made me sit through PowerPoint presentations on what to do if I'm kidnapped and held for ransom," I replied.

To my surprise, the Big Bad Wolf burst out laughing. "You've got to be kidding."

"Why would I lie? What would I gain from it?"

"A PowerPoint? Seriously?"

"PowerPoints are useful ways to present information. That's what you're going to get hung up on right now?" Nothing in that presentation prepared me for this.

"Did the presenter get any of it right?"

"The chain part lives up to its reputation." To punctuate my point, I shook my ankle. The chain rattled against the chair leg. "Everything else is… not what I expected."

"At the end of this kidnapping, I'd request that you fill out a short survey so we may improve our kidnappings in the future."

I wanted to laugh. Lord help me, I wanted to laugh, but I held it in. "You didn't happen to get any alcohol, did you?"

"For me. Not you."

"Rude. I'm knocking points off for that."

"Somehow, I think I'll live." His smile was unfairly charming. "What do you want for dinner?"

Chapter Nine

Will

I swept past the thoroughly unrestrained—with the exception of an ankle chain—Scarlett and headed into the kitchen. When I returned, she had a suspicious look in her green eyes that seemed to suggest fear of a reprisal for her escape attempt.

"Here," I handed her the sack. "I got you a few different dresses. Should be a little warmer, and cover more, than what you have on now."

"Or more aptly, what I don't have on," she peeked inside the bag with visible distaste. Her gaze rose sharply to meet my own. "You picked these out?"

"Yeah," I said cautiously. "What's wrong? Are they ugly?"

"No," she arched her crimson brows, her cute face adopting a pleased expression. "Actually, they're really pretty. You're good at picking out girls' clothes, Big Bad Wolf."

I grunted noncommittally and headed into the kitchen. "I'll keep my back turned if you want to change."

"Haven't you pretty much seen everything I have anyway?" she called from the living room.

I dropped a package of chicken breasts on the floor, cursing my sudden clumsiness. A memory of her naked pussy sprang unbidden into my mind, and I had to shake my head in an effort to clear the images.

"That was incidental, part of the job," I called back. "I won't take advantage of you in that way."

"Oh, incidental?" Her voice teemed with stiff resentment. "I see. So, when we were dancing, and I rubbed my ass all over your cock, it got hard for incidental reasons? And that make out session—that *hot as all hell* make out session in the quiet room—that was incidental and meaningless, too?"

I thought, *What in the hell is her game?* But her voice seemed so sincerely hurt that I had to do something.

Peeking my head out around the door separating the kitchen and living space, I found her staring at me with venom in those emerald eyes. "I admit there were some blurred lines there."

"Blurred lines?" she laughed. "You were *mauling* me in that quiet room. Are you that good of an actor, or was there some chemistry there? Because *I* wasn't acting."

My mouth went suddenly dry, my mind practically broken by her line of inquiry. Again, I tried to convince myself this was all an elaborate ruse on her part, an attempt to get me to let my guard down long enough so she could escape.

Yet, she seemed so sincere, so… enticing. I couldn't help myself with my response.

"There was chemistry," I growled like the Wolf she called me. "There is chemistry. Do you want me to say that I haven't been able to stop thinking about that quiet room since we left? Because I can't."

A smile spread across her lips, and she stood up with a rattling of her ankle chain. "Good. Believe it or not, that makes this all a lot easier."

She reached down and lifted the hem of her outfit over her head, exposing her naked body to me fully for the first time. My jaw dropped open, and I grew instantly, painfully erect before I forced myself to turn away.

With shaking hands, I struggled to unpack the rest of the groceries. The image of her freckled, gloriously curved body remained stuck firmly in my mind's eye. The rattling of chains from the other room seemed to suggest she'd finished dressing and sat once more, but I resisted the urge to peek.

As I selected an appropriate-sized saucepan, I again heard the rattle of her chain as she walked to the door of the kitchen. There was enough slack that she could make it all the way to the floating island. When I turned to face her, she wore the calico dress I'd purchased for her and a wide smile on her freckled face.

"So, what's on the menu? Steak and potatoes? Raw meat? A helpless little bunny? How does the Big Bad Wolf sate his hunger?"

I glanced at her with a raised eyebrow. "Chicken parmesan with sautéed mushrooms and asparagus, and cannoli for dessert."

Her green gaze widened as she leaned her elbows on the island and fixed me with an inscrutable gaze. "Wow. Color me impressed. Mind if I watch?"

"You're already watching," I pointed out.

"Mmm, yes, but you're in charge here, not me." She batted her eyelashes. I wondered if that was even true or not. Scarlett had a power over me that was both profound and irresistible, no matter what I may have told myself.

"You can watch," I answered lamely, turning away from those smoldering, intense eyes.

"What are you doing?" I heard a hint of alarm in her voice.

"I'm making dinner." I didn't turn around.

"No, you big goof, I mean what are you doing specifically? To the chicken?"

I frowned, looking away from my task. "I'm marinating it in buttermilk for a few minutes. Breasts don't have much fat, so I'm trying to ensure the meat is succulent and moist."

Scarlett pursed her lips and then grinned. "Some breasts have a lot of fat." She leaned back and gestured toward her double D rack.

Sweat beaded on my brow, and it had nothing to do with working over a hot stove.

I went back to work, setting down two glass casserole pans and then three bowls. Flour for a dredge went into the second bowl, while breadcrumbs went in the third. I cracked four eggs into the first and beat them into a slurry.

"You look like you actually know what you're doing." Scarlett sounded impressed. "Don't tell me… you had to do this kidnapping to pay for your culinary school."

I laughed, actually laughed, for the first time in what felt like forever. Part of my mind screamed that I was letting her inside my head, but I ignored the voice. It was easier and easier to forget that Scarlett was my captive. That was a dangerous line of thought, but at the time, I was having too much fun to stop myself.

"No. I'm not so lucky to have had high-level training. My nonna used to babysit me when I was kid, and since I was a real handful, she put my ass to work in the kitchen. Kept me out of trouble, and I learned to cook. Fair trade."

"You were a real handful?" Her eyebrows arched over those lovely green eyes. "I have a hard time believing that."

I set the asparagus into a strainer and sprayed cold water on it for a rinse before I answered. "Why is that?"

"Well," her eyes rolled skyward as she considered her words. "I guess you're so disciplined and controlled. At least, when you're not mauling a half-naked girl at a rave party."

I dropped the colander into the sink, fortunately avoiding a spillage of its contents. Scarlett laughed. "Struck a nerve, did I?"

"You know, I can always put the ball gag back in," I muttered.

"Who says that's a deal breaker?" she teased.

I glanced sharply at her, but honestly couldn't tell if she was kidding or not. I decided there was no path forward to victory and instead changed the subject. "Do you have any food allergies?"

She seemed taken aback by the query, her smile fading. "Ah—not that I know of. I prefer to avoid things with high fructose corn syrup, but other than that, no."

"I won't purchase anything with that junk in it." I was firm on that. "I had a friend in basic training who used to swill fruit punch by the gallon. He wound up having an ulcer on his tongue."

"You were in the Army, huh?"

Fuck. I cursed myself silently for my stupidity. Some chick shakes her titties, drops some innuendo and I lose my fucking mind?

"What's wrong?" she asked after seeing my sour expression.

"Nothing," I lied, shaking my head. "Yeah, I was in the armed services. Fucking cake walk after the house I grew up in."

"Rough childhood?" She watched as I chopped the bad spots off the asparagus.

"Not really. I never wanted for anything, except maybe parental approval. I was expected to be smarter, faster, and hit harder than the other kids my age. Even a one hundred percent on an exam wasn't enough to please my father."

"What?" she asked, laughing. "What could be better than a hundred percent?"

"He just said I should have done the extra credit." I chuckled as well, spreading my arms out. "It didn't make sense to me, either, but I know he was just pushing me to be the best I could be. Isn't that what parents are supposed to do?"

"Yeah, I guess so," Scarlett sighed, eyes growing distant. "My father, well… he never expected much out of me. I guess he thought I would be a debutante trophy wife, but I wanted something more for myself."

"Maybe your podcast isn't as much about gun control as it is finding your own path, different from your father's?"

"No," she shook her head and frowned. "I mean, yes, partly, but I really do believe what I say."

"I can't agree," I replied. "I mean, if you'd had a gun, I never would have been able to snatch you."

"Think so?" Scarlett put her arms akimbo and fixed me with a stern gaze. "Even if I'd had a gun strapped to my thigh or wherever, you could still have overpowered me with ease before I could use my weapon. In fact, statistics show that the majority of the time when someone tries to use a gun for self-defense, they wind up dying at a higher rate than unarmed people."

"I don't doubt your statistics, Scarlett." I shook my head. "I do know I feel a lot better when I'm packing heat."

"Yes, but you have a dangerous livelihood," she chuckled. "Kidnapping nubile young women and dragging them off to your beach house."

"This isn't my normal gig." I was unsure why I felt the need to explain that fact.

"Really? You're quite efficient."

"I'm doing this for my family obligations," I replied, checking the temperature of the olive oil in which I was intending to fry the chicken. "It's not something I enjoy."

"Who's your family? The mob?" Another chuckle from her. When I didn't answer, she got really quiet and swallowed hard. "Oh my God, it *is* the mob."

"I never said any such thing." We're not the mob, for the record, but we do a lot of business for them.

"That's exactly what a mobster would say," she said cryptically, arching her eyebrows. It took several moments to realize she was messing with me.

Scarlett wound up helping me bread the chicken, and then I laid it into the pan carefully. The asparagus and mushrooms went into a skillet with a mix of olive oil and butter. Contrary to popular belief, butter burns at a low temperature and I didn't want that bitterness contaminating the food.

"This smells fantastic." Scarlett's belly growled so loudly I could hear it over the frying chicken. "You're very accommodating for a kidnapper, Wolf."

"Like I said, this isn't my usual gig." I turned about and fixed her with a somber gaze. "I'm sorry about all of this. None of it is your fault, all right? If I had it to do over, I'd have told De—I'd have told them to go to hell. But I didn't, and here we are."

And there I went again, almost spilling my guts. Hell, I *was* spilling my guts. I tried to tell myself I was just using Scarlett as a sounding board, an impromptu therapist. After all, she was a safe listener. She didn't even know my real name, or who I really was.

Yet, in my heart, I knew that was not the case. I was talking to her because I liked her. And no matter how hard I tried, I couldn't stow those feelings like I wanted.

Then dinner was ready. We sat down to eat, and I had no more time to pore over my thoughts.

Chapter Ten

Scarlett

"Holy shit." I couldn't help but moan as I sank my teeth into the most delicious chicken parmesan I'd ever had in my life. I couldn't remember the last time I'd eaten. It had to have been before I got ready to go to the rave. How many hours had passed since then?

"Good?" He flashed a small smile.

"Are you kidding me?" I mumbled, my mouth full. I didn't give a rat's ass if I appeared unladylike. What was my kidnapper going to do? Judge me? I'd like to see him try. He didn't have a leg to stand on. "This is fucking delicious."

I took huge bites until my plate was cleaned. "Is there more?"

"A girl with an appetite," my Wolf grinned. "How refreshing."

"Let me clear something up for you." I set down my knife and fork and propped my elbows up on the table. "All girls have appetites. For some bullshit reason, we're taught to hide it even though it's literally a basic human function. So, when some dudebro says he likes a girl with an appetite, it's actually condescending as fuck."

"Did you just call me a dudebro?" He looked like he didn't know how to handle anything I'd just said. "I don't even know what that means."

"Dudebros are the kind of idiots who think having a mother and a sister automatically makes them a feminist," I explained.

"And you think I'm one of them because I like the fact that you eat?"

"Yes. Every single human being eats. It's not a compliment."

Shit. I shouldn't mouth off to the man who kidnapped me. I mean, I'd been giving him shit (rightfully so) since he'd snatched me, but everyone had their limit. I did *not* want to find his.

"However," I cleared my throat, "this is the best chicken parm I've ever had."

"Does that cancel out the dudebro comment?" His smirk made my stomach do a funny little flutter. I told myself it was nothing more than anxiety. It definitely wasn't attraction. No way. Not a chance. Absolutely fucking not.

"We'll see."

"Maybe you'll change your mind when you taste my tiramisu." He winked.

God, he was hot. Why did he have to be so good looking? Under different circumstances, I'd be all over him. Hell, before I knew he was a bad guy, I *was* all over him.

"Did you make some?" My eyes went wide.

"No," he chuckled. "It's tricky to make. I'd rather do it in my own kitchen. This oven is kind of a piece of crap."

"You cook a lot when you're not kidnapping rich women?"

"When I can," he replied without missing a beat. "It's the only way I have full control over what I put in my body."

There's something I'd like to put in my body. I couldn't stop myself from forming the thought. The resulting blush didn't go unnoticed by the Wolf.

"Are you all right?" He flashed a knowing grin. I swore the bastard could read my mind.

"I need to shower," I blurted.

"What?"

"Um, something in your trunk got all over me." At the time, I'd been too freaked out to notice. Then, I'd been too preoccupied with making sure I didn't die and getting out of my bindings. Now, I was all too aware of something dried and kind of sticky on my right arm and side. "It's disgusting. I won't sleep like this."

"I have a feeling you aren't going to sleep anyway."

The blush on my cheeks deepened by another few shades. If he noticed, he didn't let on.

"Yeah, there's a shower." He focused on my request. "But it's not big enough for two."

"Excuse me?"

"You don't think I'm going to let you into a room all by yourself, do you?" By the stern look on his face, I knew he wasn't joking. "You seem like the wily type who would shatter a bathroom mirror in order to stab me with a piece of glass."

"I would never!" I gasped. Though, if I was being honest with myself, it wasn't that bad of an idea. I didn't think I could actually stab someone, though. Even though he kidnapped me, I wasn't sure if the Big Bad Wolf deserved a shard of glass in the belly.

I could probably knock him out with something, especially if there was some kind of guarantee I wouldn't give him brain damage. That seemed fair. I knew he didn't knock me out to kidnap me, but he did carry me through a rave with all of my lady bits on full display.

The memory sent a flush through my body. Partially from embarrassment, but other feelings were mixed in as well. The thought of being on display like that, for anyone to see, was almost… invigorating.

"You good?" the Big Bad Wolf asked. "I was only kidding about the glass thing."

"I know," I said quickly. Too quickly. "So, can I shower or what?"

"Not alone."

"I'm not showering with you!"

"I never said that." He put his hands up in mock defense. That stupid half-grin on his face told me he knew *exactly* what he'd implied. "I'll have to sit on the bathroom floor or something."

"So you can peek at me like the creep you are? No way." I folded my arms over my chest, accidentally drawing attention to my cleavage. The Big Bad Wolf's eyes darted to my tits. He didn't even try to hide it.

"Then what do you propose? I'm not removing your chain. I'll keep hold of the end while you shower. You think I don't know you'll try to make a run for it the second you're free?"

Honestly, the thought hadn't occurred to me. It wasn't that I didn't *want* to get out of here. I most definitely did. But my Wolf told me that no harm would come to me. Maybe it was wishful thinking. Maybe I was just naïve. But I believed him.

If that belief kept me from falling apart, it was worth it.

"Sit in the hall," I finally said.

He tipped his head, considering the length of the chain. "I think that would work. It might be hard for you to turn in the shower though. I'd hate for you to get tangled."

"Why do you have to say things like *that*," I groaned before I could stop myself.

"Like what?" he asked, the picture of innocence. Images flashed in my mind of him tying me up in all kinds of ways, but I pushed them away.

"Nothing. Just let me shower for fuck's sake. All right?"

"All right." He stood from the table. Before I could move, he made it all the way to the bathroom door. "You coming or what?" He yanked on my chain. Not hard. All I felt was a slightly unpleasant tugging at my ankle.

"What's your hurry?" I called back. "You have somewhere to be?"

"Yeah. Bed. I'm fucking exhausted. Do you have any idea how much jobs like this take out of me?"

"Oh, you poor baby," I hissed. "This must be just so awful for you."

At least he had the decency to look embarrassed. "I realize now that was a stupid thing to say."

"No kidding," I scoffed.

"But are you going to shower or what?"

"Yes." With an eye roll, I pushed away from the dinner table and made my way to the bathroom door. I stepped into the bathroom. It wasn't very large, but holy shit, it was *nice*. "Is that a jacuzzi tub?"

"Is it?" He shrugged. "I didn't check."

As good as a piping hot jacuzzi bath sounded, I wasn't sure I wanted to be trapped in a tub of water with the Big Bad Wolf at the door. Before I could reach the tub, the chain around my ankle went taut. I turned around to find my Wolf holding the chain with a shit-eating grin on his face.

"Seriously?" I groaned. "What the fuck?"

"I'm sorry!" He laughed. "You're fun to mess with. Your eyes literally flash when you're angry. It's adorable."

"Maybe I *will* break the bathroom mirror," I muttered. "We'll see how tough you are then."

"Even if you did, I'm sure I could wrestle the glass shards away from you. You have tiny wrists."

I held up my unbound wrists and examined them. "They aren't that tiny."

"Please! I could snap your wrist in a heartbeat if I wanted to."

I went deathly still as I tried to figure out if that was a threat or not. The Wolf's eyes widened as he realized what he'd just said. "Not that I would!" he stammered. "I wouldn't do that."

"Sure."

"Seriously," he insisted. "The ransom goes down if you're damaged."

"Damaged?" I shrieked. The Wolf laughed. A playful gleam sparkled in his eye.

"I'm kidding," he laughed. "Well, not really. What I mean is, I'm not going to damage you. You're going to walk out of here completely unscathed."

"And you're going to walk out moderately wealthy?" I shot back.

"Well, yes," he nodded. "That's the idea. I didn't kidnap you for pocket change, now did I?"

I frowned, unsure how I should respond.

"Think of it this way." He released the chain so I could reach the tub. "If your daddy forks over the agreed upon amount, he has that much less money to funnel into creating bigger, badder weapons."

I opened my mouth to argue but stopped. "That's a damn good point."

"Exactly. Now get in the shower. I don't want to spend my whole night in this hallway. I wasn't kidding when I told you I was tired."

"And I'm not kidding when I say I couldn't care less," I shot back. I yanked my chain as hard as I could. It nearly slipped out of his hands before he caught it.

"Watch it," he warned, his voice low and hard.

"I just wanted a little more slack," I replied. "If you're not careful, I'm going to slip in the shower trying to move. If I break my neck, how much money will you get?"

"Just shower." He sighed, yet he still remained in the doorway.

"Well," I prompted.

"What?"

"Look away, you fucking weirdo."

"I've seen everything there is to see." His lazy, sexy smile made me want to pull him into the shower with me, but I resisted the urge.

"You won't be seeing it again anytime soon. Turn around!"

Chuckling, he moved to the side with his back to me. All I could see was his shoulder and arm.

I turned on the water. The shower head wasn't the best. It spurted mist before actual water started coming out. Even though the knob was turned toward the hottest setting, the water was ice cold.

"This place has hot water, right?" I asked.

"Yup," he called back. "It just takes a minute. Be patient, if you know what that is."

"I'm anxious to be rescued from a kidnapper and suddenly I'm impatient?"

"Your words," he replied with a chuckle.

"Shut up."

When the water was hot enough, I undressed but kept a close eye on the door to make sure the Big Bad Wolf wasn't spying on me. As I removed my top, releasing my breasts, I realized I *almost* wanted him to look. I wanted to torment him just a tiny bit.

He never looked, though I could tell he was holding his entire body tense.

Along the top wall of the shower, opposite the door, was a long window. It was placed high enough so no one would be able to see in. The glass was marbled to obscure visibility further. As I examined the window, I realized it wasn't as narrow as it looked. I *might* be small enough to fit through it if I could get rid of the chain around my ankle.

I looked around the shower, my heartbeat quickening with each passing moment.

The shower was stocked with a bar of soap and nothing else. Didn't they realize a woman was going to be held captive here? We needed more than just a bar of soap! That shit was going to wreak havoc on my skin.

I grabbed the soap. It slipped from my fingers the moment it was wet.

Holy shit.

Before the Big Bad Wolf could notice, I worked the soap into a lather and rubbed it all over my ankle. The chain was fitted but not tight. I had some wiggle room to work with.

As I tried to pull my foot loose, the metal cuff cut into my skin. It hurt like a bitch, and tears welled in my eyes. I bit down on my lip to keep from screaming. I just had to push through the pain. I'd spent twelve hours in six-inch heels once. I could handle this.

After a lot of twisting, rubbing, and swearing under my breath, my ankle slipped free from the chain. I slipped the chain over the bathtub faucet to keep it from going slack. Carefully and quietly, I stepped onto the rim of the bathtub so I was level with the window.

It slid open without much effort. Whoever set this place up probably assumed I'd never fit. Little did they know I did regular juice cleanses to keep slim and soak up the health benefits. Dumbasses.

All I needed to do now was climb. With any luck, I'd be free within minutes.

Chapter Eleven

Will

"What's taking so long?" Leaning against the door, I rapped my knuckles against its wooden surface. When I didn't get a reply, I pressed my ear against the door, but the only thing I could hear was the steady splash of the water. "If you don't say anything," I growled, "I'm going to—*what the fuck?*"

I gave the chain a tug, but it didn't offer any resistance. The anklet clanked across the tiles until it hit the other side of the door, and that's when I realized what had happened. Gritting my teeth, I turned the door handle and burst into the bathroom.

The shower was still on, a thick cloud of steam covering the room, but there was no sign of Scarlett. My Little Red Riding Hood had escaped. My eyes darted straight toward the small window near the ceiling, barely a slit, and I shook my head as I saw the frame hanging open.

Far too large to fit through that window, I turned on my heel and rushed out of the bathroom toward the front door.

Outside, the dark blanket of night had fallen, leaving nothing but a pale full moon to light the way. A stone's throw from where I stood, I heard the waves rolling onto the sand, their steady rhythm reminding me I had to keep my cool. Scarlett couldn't have gotten far.

Running around the house, I only stopped once I was standing underneath the bathroom's window. Tiny footprints marked the place where Scarlett had landed, and the trampled weeds just a few yards away were a clear indicator of the path she had taken. It didn't take me more than two minutes of following her trail to come upon her.

"Ah, shit," I muttered under my breath, spotting her in the distance. She was running fast, her naked body backlit by the moon, but I could tell she had no idea where she was going. The direction she had chosen would only take her even farther away from civilization. Without bothering to give her a shout, I just shook my head and broke into a run.

Despite my weight, my footsteps were light, and only a trained soldier would have noticed me coming. Breathing hard, the thunderous pounding of her own heart probably made her deaf to the world at large. She never stood a chance.

"Where, exactly, do you think you're going?" Reaching out, I wrapped my fingers around her wrist and reeled her in. She gasped, her eyes widening with shock as her naked body crashed against me. Locking my eyes on hers, I sighed. "That wasn't smart."

"Let go of me," she hissed, hammering her tiny fists against my chest. As she did, her breasts swayed violently, and that was enough for my cock to twitch. The cold had made her nipples hard, their rosy color drawing me in, and I had to suck in a deep breath to regain my focus.

"Let's get you back," I told her and picked her up. She was as light as a feather, and even though she did her best to fight me off, her movements were useless. "Help! Someone, help!" she continued screaming at the top of her lungs, her voice loud enough for my eardrums to protest. Still, I didn't bother with shutting her up. As annoying as her screams were, there was no one around this place for miles. At least, not this late at night.

Once I got back to the house, I climbed up the stairs onto the porch. The entry door was still ajar and I pushed it open with the tip of my boot. I locked it behind me, and only then did I set Scarlett down.

"You're a monster," she threw at me, anger flashing in her eyes. I didn't return her gaze. Instead, I let my eyes wander down her naked body, a scorching heat taking over me as I focused on that pink flush right between her legs. When she realized I was staring at her, she covered herself with her hands, her palms over her naked pussy as the crook of her elbows squeezed her breasts together.

Her hair was still wet, locks of it plastered against her cheeks, and her teeth already chattered. The skin of her arms was prickled, and the tips of her fingers had turned pale.

"You're going to get sick." Turning my back to her, I grabbed a ratty blanket from the couch. Carrying it in my hands, I headed toward Scarlett. Reacting on instinct, she started padding backward until she hit the wall behind her. "Calm down, will ya? I'm not going to punish you or anything."

Not that I wouldn't like to turn you over my knee, I thought, imagining how it'd feel to slap that smooth backside of hers. I could see her in my mind's eyes, bent over my knees as her quivering little voice filled the air once my hand made contact. Fuck, who knew that I had such a good imagination? My cock seemed to agree with the sentiment, as it already strained against the fabric of my boxers, eager to be let loose.

"Why don't you just let me go?" she whispered, her eyes locked on mine. She ran her tongue over her bottom lip, and I caught a glimpse of her perfect white teeth. "My father is never going to pay whatever ransom you're asking. Please, just let me go."

"We've gone over this." Taking one more step forward, I draped the blanket over her naked shoulders, my thumbs brushing against the skin on her neck. An electric jolt rushed up my spine, and that's when my cock became as hard as it had ever been. A storm of lust rose inside me, and my heart kicked and punched against my ribcage, every single fiber of my being desperate for her body. "You're not going anywhere, so sit down and try to get warm."

There was a moment of silence, and I could almost feel the electricity crackling around us. Then she squared her shoulders and straightened her back. Her breasts spilled free from the hold she had on them, and the blanket slid down from her shoulders. Standing there in all of her nakedness, she gave me a defiant glare. By now, the color had started returning to her cheeks, a pink flush decorating her face.

"I'm not afraid of you," she breathed out, her words heavy, almost solemn.

"Maybe you should be," I whispered, taking one more step forward. Now, I towered over her. She kept holding my gaze, tilting her head back so she could keep our stares locked. I noticed she had balled her hands into tiny fists, but it didn't look like she wanted to fight me.

No, it looked like she wanted to…

Reaching for her, I took my fingers to her neck, enjoying the way the warmth of her skin seeped into mine. Slowly, I wrapped my fingers around the slim column, careful not to choke her. I just wanted her to know that I was in charge here. Not that she didn't know it already.

She didn't make a move.

She simply stared into my eyes, lips slightly parted. I could feel her heartbeat on the vein that crawled up her neck, its tempo more and more furious with each passing second, and my heart settled into that same rhythm.

"What do you want?" I whispered, my words dipping into half a growl. "Do you want me to punish you? Is that it?" Slowly, I leaned in so that my eyes were level with hers. Her cherry lips glistened, and something about her mouth drew me in. Before I even knew it, my face was no more than a few inches away from hers.

"I want…" She breathed out, her words scattered and loose, but she never finished her sentence. "I want you to…" Her eyes escaped my gaze, and she looked straight at my mouth. In her face, I saw longing. Desire. Raw and unadulterated.

"You want me to…?" Slowly, I closed the distance between us until our lips were almost touching. I kept a microscopic gap between them, and her eyelids fluttered gently as her heartbeat shot up through the roof. Then, before I knew what the hell I was doing, I put my free hand between her legs. I flattened my palm there, cupping her little pussy, and felt her inner lips slick with her juices. "Say it."

"I…"

"Say it."

Her eyes grew wide, and she grew wetter than I've ever felt any woman become. I could feel her fluids dripping down her inner thighs, all of her lust and desire now coating my fingers.

"Take me," she finally breathed out, all of her fears and hesitation hiding behind her words. The Scarlett she pretended to be didn't want for this to happen, but the *true* Scarlett—the one whose soul was brimming with dark desires—craved it. She was hungry for it.

"I will," I whispered, "but I want to hear you say it."

"Fuck me."

Her words slipped out from between her lips fast, blending into a single sound, and her whole body seemed to melt. The tension that had pooled in her shoulders vanished, and even her knees seemed to buckle. Then, she finally closed her eyes and tipped herself forward, crushing her lips against mine. We kissed.

I parted her lips with the tip of my tongue, the taste of ripe strawberries and feminine lust flooding my mouth, and I peeled my fingers away from her neck. Placing both hands on her waist, I kept her pinned against the wall as our kiss deepened. She moaned softly against my lips, pressing her naked breasts against my chest, and I couldn't help but grin as I felt her hard nipples brushing against my shirt.

I pulled back from her, but my hands remained where they belonged. Digging my fingers into her soft flesh, I let my mouth wander down her neckline, my tongue caressing her warm skin. I kept going until I was savoring the rising curve of her breast, and I only stopped once I had sucked her left nipple into my mouth. I twirled my tongue around it, enjoying its hardness, and then whipped at it as furiously as I could.

She moaned again, this time louder, and her voice echoed throughout the empty house. Needing to hear more of it, I took my hand to her wetness again and draped my thumb over her clit. She tensed, her body electrified by desire.

"Oh, God," she breathed out, tilting her head back.

"God?" Straightening myself, I smiled. Then, I pushed her hair away from her face and brushed my lips against her right ear. "There's no God here, Scarlett. It's just me." Without missing a beat, I started stroking her clit with my thumb, and her mouth hung open in a cry of silent agony. Unable to restrain herself, completely lost in the throes of pleasure, she allowed a wicked smile to dance on her lips.

She was a good girl. The kind of girl who would help an elderly lady cross the street, pay for a homeless man to get back on his feet, and stand up against whatever injustice she might find on her way home. She was a good girl, the kind who tidied her bedroom every night, just like her mom taught her to.

Thing is, every good girl has a shadow, and Scarlett's shadow was jet black. No matter what she told herself, she wanted a man like me. No, she *needed* a man like me. She wanted to be bent over and ravaged, to feel as if she had no control over her body. She wanted me to take over every fiber of her being and drown her in as much pleasure as she could take.

She was in luck.

After all, I was more than willing to oblige.

Chapter Twelve

Scarlett

I couldn't believe what was happening.

With my head thrown back, I bit the inside of my cheeks to keep myself silent. I felt the sharp stab of pain on my flesh, but I didn't feel the dream I was in collapsing in on itself. Instead, the pain just reminded me that what was happening was real.

"Fuck," I breathed out, his mouth returning to my breasts. His tongue danced around my nipple for a moment, and then it wandered to my other breast in a slow and maddening motion.

No, my inner voice shouted, *this isn't you, Scarlett! Put a stop to it! Don't let this monster—*

"I want you to fuck me," I repeated, enjoying the way the words rolled off my tongue. Grinning, I choked out my inner voice and sat my instincts behind the steering wheel. Not that it mattered who was driving. I was like a ship without a rudder, my fate in the hands of the ocean.

"I'm going to do more than just fuck you." He stared up at me with the devil's smile. The lines on his face had deepened, almost as if the lust swirling inside me had made him even wilder than he already was, and my heart tightened as I accepted just how attracted to him I was. He made me angry, afraid… but he also made me as wet as I had ever been.

With his hands on my hips, he kept me in place as his mouth wandered farther south, his lips now trailing toward my stomach.

"What are you—?"

"Stay still," he growled, his deep voice and commanding tone enough for me to do as I was told. I just threw my weight against the wall behind me, my lungs struggling to gather air, and let his mouth roam over my naked skin. He opened his hands, his fingers slowly stretching over my hips, and then slid them over to my ass. Digging his fingertips into my flesh, he kissed my inner thighs, the smooth way in which he did it leaving me crazed with lust.

"Lift your leg," he commanded as he dropped to one knee, and my body reacted before my mind could register his words. I did as I was told, and he helped me rest the back of my knee over his shoulder. A grin tugged at the corner of his lips, his eyes focused on the aching wetness between my legs, and that's when he leaned forward.

I chomped my bottom lip as he traced the contour of my inner lips with his tongue, over and over again, and my eyes rolled as I tried to process all that was happening. Slowly, and not sure if I was allowed to, I laid both hands on his head, gently threading my fingers into his hair. He said nothing.

"You should've told me you were this delicious," he whispered, the way the air moved past his lips as he spoke making my skin prickle. Perhaps sensing my anticipation, he flicked his tongue up and twirled it around my clit. I shut my eyes, ecstasy coursing through my veins like a drug, and gasped as he finally wrapped his lips around my tiny bud.

Suddenly, he opened his mouth wide and pressed it against my aching pussy, his tongue furiously whipping at my clit. I went from gasping to moaning, and from that to screaming, my voice taking flight and filling the entire room. I felt my vocal cords vibrating like the strings of a violin, and I wouldn't have been surprised if I heard every window on this place shatter. That, of course, didn't happen.

Instead my legs trembled, my heart beating a thousand miles per hour, and my brain felt as if it had melted in my skull. I'm pretty sure had anyone asked me for my name then and there, that I wouldn't have been able to answer the question. The only thing I knew was that my body was electrified with desire, and every nerve ending inside me turned and bloomed like a sunflower.

"That feels so…"

I gasped as he brushed two fingers against my entrance, his fingertips caressing my folds. Slowly, he eased them in, curling them upward as if they were a hook. Then he drove them all the way into me, only stopping when he had them pressed against that hidden trigger inside. It only took a couple of seconds for fireworks to go off behind my shut eyelids.

My thoughts scattered like birds taking flight, and I took a breath so deep that I felt my lungs pushing against my ribcage. Balling my hands into fists, I yanked on his hair and pushed his mouth against my drenched pussy while, at the same time, I thrust against him.

I came, and I came *hard*.

My muscles tensed, becoming heavy as concrete, and I let out a quivering moan. Pleasure turned into sound, electric ecstasy crackling under my skin, and my knees buckled under my weight. Moving fast, he laced one hand around my waist, keeping me upright. When he pulled back from me, I forced my eyes open and looked down to meet his dark gaze. His chin glistened from my juices, the sight of it making my heart do a somersault inside my chest, and that's when I realized just how desperate I was for his touch.

"More," I told him, my voice brimming with that desperation. "I want more."

"Do you?" he threw back at me, but what he really wanted to say was, "Of course you want more." And he was right. Every gesture I made, every breath I took... all made it painfully obvious just how much I wanted him. "You try to play the role of a good girl, but in truth..." Standing up, he brushed two fingers—the same fingers he had just had inside me—against my cheek. "You're a dirty girl. You want to be fucked, and you want to be fucked hard."

"Yes..." I replied, forcing myself to acknowledge that savagery that lay hidden inside my soul. It felt as if I'd broken the chains of decency and decorum, and I loved every second. Oh, I wasn't exactly a prude, and I had had my share of hot and sweaty flings. This, though, was something else entirely. To be with him made me feel free, as if there were no limitations to what I could do. "I want to be fucked hard... by *you*."

"You're in luck," he whispered, taking my hand and placing it right between his legs. I turned my wrist, and slowly, I wrapped my fingers around his hard shape. My breath caught in my throat as, once more, I felt his thickness. I knew some men were well-endowed, but that was just ridiculous. "Right now, I want nothing more than to make you scream, Scarlett."

"Then what are you waiting for?" Tightening my fingers around his cock, I stroked him over the fabric of his pants, my pace rapid and furious. Using my free hand, I pulled his shirt over his head and then ran my fingers over his wall of abs, feeling every groove and ridge of his muscles. His body was perfection made flesh, almost as if God himself had grabbed a chisel and decided to carve him into existence, just so he could have the perfect example of how a man should look.

His muscles were pure slabs of power and functionality, every inch of his skin brimming with raw savagery. In this modern age, most men with muscles tended to look like gym rats, their proportions a result of notebooks of carefully planned workouts and hours of counting carbs, but my Wolf… I know it seemed silly, but it felt like he had never set foot inside a gym. He had the kind of body that made it easy to believe he had earned by chopping wood and hunting wild animals with his bare hands.

It was the body of a *predator*. And I was his prey.

Gritting my teeth, my heart ramming itself against its cage, I unbuckled his belt and pulled it free from its loops. After the whooshing sound of the leather slipping free, he kicked off his boots. As he threw his pants to the side, I couldn't stop myself from looking down, the hard shape tenting his boxer briefs looking more like a sledgehammer than a cock. Jesus fucking Christ, how could he be this big? Was he even going to fit inside me?

"Don't worry," he whispered into my ear, almost as if he had opened a window into my mind and was peering inside it. "I'm going to be gentle. Or, well, I'll try. No promises."

Running his hands down the side of my body, his touch letting me know I was his, he slammed me back against the wall. Then, with one quick movement, he pulled me up and into him. I reacted on instinct, lacing my legs around his waist and throwing my arms over his shoulders as he rested his body against mine.

With my breasts mashed to his chest, my hard nipples feeling like sharp razors, I threw my head back and readied myself for what was to come. I felt the tip of his hard cock against my inner lips, and I knew that he was just a thrust away from—

"Holy fuck," I cried out, thunder and lightning exploding inside me as he thrust. His long inches slid inside me fast, his massive cock stretching me wide on the way in. For a moment, it almost felt like he was going to split me in half. His promises of gentleness seemed to have been thrown out of the window and thank God. A man with a cock like this should never have to be gentle.

"You're so fucking tight," he growled, a devilish smile on his lips. Placing one hand on the nape of my neck, he threaded his fingers into my hair and held my head up, forcing me to look straight into his eyes. "I can tell you've never been with a real man."

With that, he slid his cock out until only his tip was inside of me, and then he slammed it back in. I moaned and, Jesus, I did it so hard that it felt like my vocal cords were going to snap.

Pistoning into me, his movements charged with furious lust, he drove me up into new heights. I soared over my own consciousness, my nerve endings burning from the inside out, and I surrendered my whole body to him. No, not just my body—even my soul had kneeled down in front of him, begging him to own it.

"I think I'm going to—"

I didn't finish my sentence.

His thrusts silenced me, and the muscles in my neck felt like a vise around my throat. Perhaps feeling it, he took one hand to my neck and wrapped his fingers around it, choking me in the most delicious of ways. It made me feel as if I was being stripped of my own free will and, against all odds and common sense, I couldn't stop myself from loving every second of it.

"Come," he whispered into my ear, the gentleness in his voice contrasting with the viciousness of his movements.

Thrusting even harder than before, his movements threatening to ruin my pussy for all other men, he led me straight to the edge. One quick push and I tumbled down from pleasure's cliff and, for a moment, it felt as if the universe was folding into itself.

Blinding light exploded on the edges of my vision and my thoughts turned into ash as a tidal wave of pleasure crashed against me. Hard spasms took over my inner walls, and they became as tight as a vise, choking his hard cock; still, he didn't let that stop him. Instead, he just doubled up on the viciousness of his thrusts, his cock like a battering ram. I screamed until I no longer knew if I was still doing it, or if what I was hearing was just the echo of my own voice.

"So fucking good," he growled, and with one final thrust, he finally stopped all movement. His shoulders rounded up, his muscles bulging under the skin. For a moment, he was made of marble. Even his cock became as hard as a slab of concrete. When it throbbed, it felt like an earthquake happening inside me, and my mind spun as he spilled his seed inside me.

We didn't move for a long time.

We just remained locked in that embrace, basking in the glory of what we had just done. Breathing hard, I felt like the dirtiest girl that had ever walked the earth, one capable of stepping over the limits of what was reasonable and acceptable. I mean, sex with my own kidnapper?

It was crazy, and I absolutely loved it.

Chapter Thirteen

Will

Warm, soft light filtered through the boards over the bedroom window, turning the view of my eyelids from black to red. Stubbornly, I rolled over, away from the sun, nestling myself into the blankets more fully. My hand reached out to caress the equally warm and soft body on the bed next to me…

And patted about, finding nothing. Nothing but furrowed, rumpled sheets. My eyes snapped open at the same time as my heartrate jumped up a thousand percent in tempo.

Scarlett was gone. After our wild, passionate screw last night, I'd forgotten to re-attach her ankle chain.

No, I thought bitterly as I threw the covers off my naked form and leaped to my feet. No, I hadn't forgotten. I had chosen not to do so, despite the fact that it was clearly not a good idea.

What in the hell had I been thinking? I was supposed to be a professional, yet I fell for the oldest trick in the book and let myself be seduced by a target. This was Hollywood bullshit, not real life.

And unlike a Hollywood movie, when a client fucked a guy, they also fucked a guy over. How far did she get? Was she at the police precinct right now? Did I need to burn out of here in a hurry?

As I headed out into the hall, too frantic to dress myself, I started considering my options. I wasn't lying to her when I said I had a rock-solid alibi backed up by cell data. My cousins were up there now, carrying a dupe phone around to make sure I was covered.

But still... Devlin and the others would never forgive me. They might even decide that in order to protect the firm's reputation they would have to see that I took a vacation—the *permanent* kind.

Halfway down the stairs to the relatively uncluttered first floor, the smell hit my nostrils. Burning. Something was burning.

Scarlett, you little... Did you set the fucking house on fire? Such were my thoughts as I reached the first floor.

But then I heard the faucet running, and my anger turned to confusion. Who in the hell was in the kitchen?

I popped around the corner, my eyes staring daggers until they settled upon Scarlett's freckled, shapely back, exposed because the only thing she wore was my apron. She cursed as she poured batter into a hot skillet, sending up a cloud of smoke and increasing the burned smell. Something charred and unrecognizable lay on the plate next to her.

"What are you doing?" My voice came out a bit harshly because I wasn't over my scare. Scarlett jumped and dropped the spatula on the floor before turning around to face me.

"You scared the shit out of me, Wolf," she smiled.

"Are you trying to make pancakes?" I looked at the box of mix and bottle of syrup sitting on the floating island.

"Yeah, emphasis on *trying*," she laughed. Scarlett gestured helplessly to the mess she'd made. She filled out the apron damn well, that was for certain. Her creamy bosom enticed my gaze, the pinkness of her areolas sticking out, and she'd belted the waist tightly enough to accentuate her generous curves. Her red tresses had been pinned back by a scrunchie to form a ponytail, leaving the back of her neck bare and displaying the hickeys I'd left there last night.

"Get that pan off the hot burner." I called out before retreating and grabbing some clothes from my nearby duffel. Clothed in jeans and a t-shirt, I returned to the kitchen and opened a drawer, selecting a fresh pan. "Did you put any oil on the pan?"

"No…" Scarlett said sheepishly. "I put a pat of butter."

"Butter burns at a low temperature, much lower than you need to cook pancakes. Use coconut oil instead."

She stood aside while I took over the process of preparing our breakfast. My mind still raced with questions. Why didn't she leave when she had the chance? Was this all some sort of game to her?

My thoughts turned ever more elaborate and paranoid. *Perhaps*, I thought, *Scarlett already left and called the authorities, and returned just to keep me here in place until they arrived?*

No, I thought, that made no sense. Why risk herself coming back here if she was safe? But if this wasn't some sort of trick, what the hell was she up to?

I refused to entertain, even for a second, the idea that Scarlett had remained out of some sort of burgeoning feelings for me on a personal level. I tried to force these thoughts away and concentrate on making the food. Scarlett hovered right by my side, her body heat and scent driving me wild.

"Did you even read the recipe?" I sniffed the messy bowl of batter sitting on the counter. It seemed oddly flat and lifeless for pancake batter.

"Uh, I thought it was just add water." She gestured at the bowl.

"I see. Unfortunately, this isn't instant mix. One needs to add in oil and eggs in addition to the water."

"You have to add oil and eggs? Then what's the point of the mix?"

I paused with the fridge door standing wide open, considering her query. Wait, what was the point of the mix? Baking powder. That's all I could come up with at the time. "I guess… we don't have to measure baking powder," I shrugged.

She laughed, which made her chest dance in most alluring ways. Then she trotted over to me and stood, hands clasped behind her back, eyes glittering up at me.

"What?" I demanded, one hand on the carton of eggs, the other bearing milk.

Suddenly she got up on her tiptoes and kissed me on the lips. A full, intense kiss, plenty of tongue probing, which I returned in kind. Suddenly I wasn't so worried about my paranoia…

She broke away and then slapped me on the chest playfully. "Get to work, bitch. I'm hungry."

I gaped at her in astonishment, and then we both burst into laughter. We measured out the mix, and then added in a greasy dollop of coconut oil and two eggs. While she beat the mix together, I checked the temperature of the skillet. Dead solid perfect.

"Do you like them silver dollar style?" I asked as she handed me the bowl.

"Hmmm, no, I like big, fluffy pancakes."

"Big and fluffy it is," I turned back to pour the mix onto the sizzling skillet. Scarlett came up behind me and encircled my naked waist with her arms.

"What are you doing?" I demanded, stiffening up.

"Nothing... yet," she said playfully. Her hand dropped down and fondled my cock. "Now I'm doing something."

"You're going to make me burn the food." My objection was weak and I made no move to stop her.

"Oh, I guess I'd better let you go then." She released her grip and backed up several feet. I turned a baleful eye on her, and she laughed and then stuck out her tongue. "Don't mess up my pancakes, bitch."

"I'll show you who's the bitch," I growled back.

"*Oooh,*" she said, her mouth forming an O, eyes glittering with delight. "Promise?"

I arched an eyebrow at her and she tilted her head slightly, as if awaiting a response. At length, she spoke again.

"Your pancakes are burning," she offered.

Cursing, I spun about and quickly scraped the flapjack off the skillet. When I flipped it over, it was a little dark but not burned, fortunately.

Soon we had a tall stack of buttermilk pancakes, a shit ton more carbs than I usually ingested in one sitting, but this was an extraordinary situation. I took a moment to appreciate the utter absurdity of cooking pancakes—naked—in the kitchen of a safe house with the same woman I abducted a day earlier. Who wore only an apron. With whom I'd had the most mind-blowing, awesome sex in my entire life the night before.

Like I said, an extreme set of circumstances. So, I figured I could have an unscheduled cheat day and eat some goddamn pancakes.

When all that was left of the flapjacks were sticky fingers and smiles, I finally broached the subject I'd avoided all morning. I stared across the counter at Scarlett and cleared my throat.

"So…"

She glanced up and saw my somber expression, her smile fading. "So… what?"

"You know what I'm getting at," my tone sharp.

"Uh, no I don't… I left my mind reading powers at the rave when you snatched me."

"Damn it," I gripped my fork tight and jabbed it in her direction. "Do I have to spell it out? You're still here."

"Yeah?" she said, growing a bit angry. "Of course, I'm still here. I'm not allowed to leave, remember? I'm your captive."

I sputtered for several seconds before I managed to speak. "You… I don't… for the love of… come on, you could have left last night after I fell asleep. I'm actually going nuts trying to figure out why you didn't."

Scarlett lowered her fork to her plate with a clatter and glared at me. "It's not that hard to figure out."

Then her expression softened, and she actually reached out and put her hand on top of mine. I stared at the freckled surface of her skin, scarcely believing what was happening even as a hard throb pulsed through my chest. Was I really getting excited over a little hand holding, after the debauchery of last evening?

"Then tell me. I'm simple."

She laughed and squeezed my hand warmly. "You're anything but simple." Scarlett sighed, and looked at me with those warm green eyes that threatened to melt my steely heart. "I just figured that I'm probably safer with you than I would be trying to run, even to the cops. I mean, if the people you work for are connected as well as you say…"

"They are, but why do you think you'd be safe with me?" I demanded. "I'm the one who kidnapped you in the first place."

"Yes, but you promised I'd walk out of here alive," she whispered, her lower lip trembling.

"And you believed me?" I asked with a snarl. For some reason I felt really angry at the moment.

"Sure," she smiled. "You're a good man, Mr. Big Bad Wolf. Even if you don't want to admit it, not even to yourself."

I stared at her, all pretty and sweet and tempting, and hated myself. I hated myself for what she made me feel and for making me doubt everything I thought I knew.

"I am not a good man," I growled. "It's time you learned that lesson. Don't trust anyone."

"I trust you."

Her tenderness only made me angrier. Snarling, I grabbed her wrist and dragged her into the living room. Scarlett stumbled after me, not resisting other than with panicked queries.

"What's wrong? Why are you so angry?"

I didn't answer, only roughly untied the apron and yanked it off her body. Then I grabbed her by the jaw and squeezed hard, drawing her face up toward mine.

"Let's see if you still think I'm good after this."

Then I shoved her down into the chair and ripped the strings off the apron with savage jerks. She watched, hurt dancing in her eyes but without an ounce of resistance as I lashed her wrists to the armrests, making the knots miserably tight. The thin fabric cut into her skin, bulging and bubbling it outward and obviously cutting off the circulation. The emotions this conjured in me only made me angrier because I didn't want to feel anything. I think I was trying to prove that she meant nothing to me by being extra cruel.

Tears welled in her green eyes, though I don't think it was from the pain of the strands binding her to the chair. I reconnected her ankle chain, doing so in a way that bound her ankles together, and then shoved the ball gag into her mouth. She groaned as I tightened it several notches more than I had before, forcing her jaws wide apart and spawning a line of drool drizzling down her chin and onto her naked body.

I stared at her as if to say, "How do you like that?" But she didn't grow angry or offer protest of any kind. She simply stared at me with those horribly hurt eyes, and I had to turn away. I ripped a strip of cloth from the nearby blanket and covered those haunting eyes.

Then I left.

I made it all the way into the car before I realized there was no way I could leave her in such a state. No matter how much I wanted to deny it, Scarlett had wormed her way into my heart.

Glumly, with an air of defeated resignation, I exited the car and headed back inside the house to set her free.

Chapter Fourteen

Scarlett

SNOT DRIBBLED DOWN MY CHIN, MIXING WITH THE DROOL spilling out of my forced-open lips as I sat in abject misery. I couldn't even move enough to wipe my face clean. My arms ached horribly from the taut apron strings, and the constant urge to swallow could not be sated or I'd wind up choking on the plastic ball wedged between my teeth.

But the physical discomfort from the cruelly tight restraints didn't lead to my despair. I was haunted by the angry, bitter light in Wolf's eyes as he'd tied me. The funny thing was, I don't think he was angry at me at all. I think his rage had been directed at himself because he felt things he couldn't understand. Things for *me*.

I could relate. The entire time I'd been around him, Wolf had a profound effect on me. Despite the insistence of many popular right-wing blogs, I was not, in fact, naïve. I didn't believe in love at first sight, or any of that fated soulmate garbage.

What I did believe in was the power of chemistry. Some people just had the right set of different charges to create sparks. It had been nothing but sparks between me and Wolf, save for my terrifying abduction and trip inside the suitcase and car trunk.

While I had not enjoyed that one bit, I had found comfort at the least in the way Wolf sought to take care of me. He saw that I was fed, had water, bathed…

My mind revolted suddenly with the thought that if I were a dog, I could list the same virtues of my owner.

I stiffened when the sound of the door, which adjoined kitchen and garage, slammed shut. Was he back already? Or was this someone else? A thought boiled in me right then—one that suggested I'd rather not be rescued. I hated myself for that thought, hated myself for desiring Wolf so badly even when he'd been so cruel.

Blindfolded, I followed the sound of his footsteps with my face anyway as he came to a halt right in front of me. His heavy breathing wafted over me, mixed with the smell of his anxious sweat. I was too afraid to make a sound, yet desperately wanted him to say something, do something. Anything, other than just stand there and torment me with his presence.

I felt his hands pull and tug at the knotted fabric around my eyes until it fell slack, dropping around my neck. Our eyes met, his dark gaze holding an unexpectedly tender light. Wolf reached for me, and I lowered my gaze to my lap so he could access the buckle on the gag.

He carefully picked out the hair that had been entangled with the leather and brass, taking pains not to hurt me, and then extracted the ball from my mouth. I worked my aching jaw, now free to speak but afraid to utter a sound. Wolf used his handkerchief to wipe my face clean of drool and mucous and then went to work untying my wrists.

Wolf winced at the sight of the red indentations left behind on my skin by the cruelly tight strands. He rubbed them gently with his fingers and then lifted his gaze to meet my own.

"I'm sorry, Scarlett." His voice was tinged with deep regret. "I—I never wanted you to get hurt. In any way."

"Then stop hurting me, Mr. Wolf." I was surprised at the conviction in my tone. "You have the power to stop at any time."

His face contorted in a guilty mask as he pondered my words. "I wish I could, but I can't let you go. Not yet."

"I know you can't, Wolf." I sighed and shifted in the chair. It was far less comfortable when my naked butt was pressed into the hard surface, and it wasn't comfortable to start. "You're trapped into your fate by your family. Like me."

I dared to lift my hand and caress his cheek. He started, flinching away. But I touched him again, caressing his skin with my soft palm. Wolf's big, hairy-knuckled hand lifted and cupped over mine, and then gently pulled it away so he could bend himself to the task of freeing my ankles.

As he turned the key in the padlock, opening its hasp, I pondered whether I should say my thoughts out loud. Watching the gentle, careful way he unwound the chains and attended to my red and sore ankles gave me enough courage to speak.

"Why did you come back?"

He looked at me in misery and shook his head, squeezing his eyes shut. "I don't even know, Scarlett. I just couldn't leave you… like that."

I thought he added the last two words on more for his benefit than for my own.

"I think you do know, Wolf." I caressed his stubbly cheek. "But you don't have to say it out loud right now if you don't want to."

"Say what?" He tried to sound harsh, but it came out a bit plaintive instead.

I just smiled and leaned forward, kissing him on his lips. He accepted it, his tongue darting inside of my mouth, but then he broke away and held me by my shoulders, staring at me hard.

"What's wrong with you?" he demanded, shaking me a little. "Why are you doing this?"

"Doing what?" My tone was sweet, my turn to be cryptic.

"You know… this." He let go of me and shook his hands about as if gesturing toward all of creation in general. "Kissing me. Sleeping with me. Not escaping when you had the chance. Is this all a game? Are you in cahoots with Devlin, trying to fuck with my head?"

"I don't know who Devlin is, Mr. Wolf," I said, growing angry and not afraid to show it in my voice. "And while I'm not averse to the idea of games—particularly the naughty kind—I assure you I'm not playing you."

"Then why?" He shook his head and crossed those massive arms over his barrel chest. "Why…"

I gasped, realizing what he was truly getting at, and astonishment filled my tone as my mouth dropped open. "You can't let yourself believe that I'm attracted to you. Can you?"

"I said no such thing." Wolf stiffened, his arms falling to his sides while his hands grasped into fists.

"You don't have to. It's written all over your face and the way you brutally tied me to the chair." I laughed and stroked my finger along the ridge of his chiseled jaw. "I can't figure out why you'd think I wouldn't be attracted to you. I mean, you look like you belong on the cover of a romance novel."

"I would think my kidnapping you and holding you hostage would have a lot to do with you not finding me attractive." Wolf arched one bushy brow.

"Yes, that would normally be a deal breaker, but… life doesn't always fit into neat little boxes." I smiled up at him, blushing a little when I realized I was still naked as a jaybird, not that he hadn't already thoroughly examined every inch of my body. "Regardless of how we met, I can't deny what I'm feeling. And neither should you."

"I—I don't have any…" Wolf's eyes squeezed tightly shut as his palms rose up to rest on either side of his head. I could see the conflict playing out in his body language and facial expressions, mirroring what was happening inside his mind. "I—I'm not *allowed* to have feelings like that. Not for someone like you."

"Someone like me?" I chuckled. "You mean, podcasters? Lefties? Naked women who don't exactly object to being tied up and manhandled under the right circumstances? Protestants? Non-Italians? Help me out here, I'm drowning."

I watched his face go through a ton of conflicting emotions at my examples. His cheeks turned red when I mentioned being sort of into the idea—if not the actual practice—of captivity, but he was stubbornly insistent upon sticking to his guns.

"No, of course not. I mean…" He turned his massive back on me, his shoulders slightly slumped. "Look, Scarlett. You and me, we're from different worlds. You get it? The world I'm from is populated with people who just aren't very nice. And you, you're… you're…"

"I'm what, Wolf?" I felt bad at his torment but at the same time wanted him to make the breakthrough I knew he could.

"Innocent." He finally turned to face me. "You're just so goddamned innocent."

"Innocent?" I burst into laughter. "After all the things we did to each other last night, you're going with *innocent*?"

"That's not what I mean," Wolf snarled. "You're a good person, Scarlett. Too good, too pure at heart for my world. I just don't see any future for us that doesn't end in tragedy."

"Then maybe you're not looking hard enough." I stood at last, walked over to him and wrapped my arms around his waist, laying my cheek on his firm chest. "Or maybe, you're just afraid to see what's right in front of you."

He sucked in a great breath, swelling his chest against my face as I heard the rapid tattoo of his beating heart. "And what is in front of me, Scarlett?" he demanded softly.

"Right now, a naked girl who's totally ready to go," I purred, nibbling on his nipple through the thin fabric of his shirt.

"You know what I mean." He gasped as my attentions had the desired effect. I could feel his bulge growing against me, heightening my own arousal. "How does this end? After the ransom is paid, I mean?"

"Once the ransom is paid, there's nothing keeping us from seeing each other." My hands slid over his chiseled back muscles.

"How would we even explain to people where we met?" he gasped, his arms encircling my waist.

"Tell them the truth—we met a rave, you got rough and kinky and one thing led to another," I murmured into his skin. His hands felt amazing as they crawled all over me, caressing my spine and cupping my buttocks firmly, kneading them and prying them wide apart.

"Oh, Scarlett," he said in sudden relief, clasping me to him even tighter. "I need you so fucking bad it's driving me crazy."

"I need you, too, Wolf," I whispered, exulting in his embrace.

"Will," he muttered into my neck as he left tender kisses there.

"What?"

"*Will*. My name is Will."

Our eyes met and then our lips, but just when I really felt swept up into the swirl of ecstasy, his phone rang. The way his body stiffened against mine let me know it was a call that was both very important and unsettling.

"I have to take this." He dug out his phone with one hand but still clasped me at the small of the back with the other. I watched his face intently as he took the call.

"Yeah?" The other person spoke, and other than the fact that it was a man, I couldn't tell anything else about what they said. "Are you kidding me? The guy's fucking loaded. Yes, of course. I'm a professional. What does that have to do with—"

Will's face grew hard, and his gaze filled with panic when he looked at me.

"Let's hope it doesn't get to that point." His voice was tight as a drum. "Fine. I'm sure he'll get the money together in a couple of days. Yeah, you're right. I'll switch to a new burner just in case." Will ended the call and stared at me for a long time before speaking. "Get dressed. We're moving to a new safe house."

"What's going on?"

"Your father needs a few days to liquefy his assets. In the meantime, we need to move just in case this location has been compromised."

"I didn't call anyone," my own tone harsh. "Even though I easily could have while you were sleeping."

"I know. I know," he assured me, caressing my face with his palm. "I know, okay? Just get dressed, please, and hurry. I have a bad feeling about this."

I nodded and went to do as he asked. But I was filled with trepidation over this unexpected move.

What kind of game was my father playing?

Chapter Fifteen

Will

Scarlett fussed with her wide-brimmed straw hat as I pulled the Cordoba out onto the highway and headed south. Her freckled face wrinkled into a frown as she adjusted her sunglasses with a painted nail.

"Do I really have to wear these?" She let loose a helpless laugh. "I mean, this hat is at least two seasons out of style. Not to mention no one wears blue-framed sunglasses anymore."

I glanced over at her sharply. The hat I'd found up in the beach house attic, but I'd picked out those sunglasses specifically for Scarlett because I thought they were pretty. It seemed I was wrong.

"I'm afraid so, Red," I grinned. "You're a missing person, and most everyone carries a cell phone in their pocket these days."

"Fine, but I don't have to like it." She peered out the window as we passed by rows of waving reeds bordering the roadside. "It's a bit windy today."

"Yes. The ocean will be choppy."

Scarlett turned her glasses-shrouded face my way, an incredulous expression marring her pretty features. "The ocean will be choppy? What does that have to do with what I said?"

I smiled cryptically and just kept driving. Scarlett leaned back in her seat and stretched like a cat.

"Oh fine, be that way." A grin teased her lips. "It's not like you have anything to gain by keeping your secrets, though. If you wanted to keep me from knowing the way to the next safe house, you'd have blindfolded me. Or tied me up and stuck me back in the trunk."

"That can be arranged," I spoke as if seriously considering it.

Scarlett turned and stuck her tongue out. "Don't threaten me with a good time. Except the trunk really sucked. The handcuffs weren't so bad, though."

I arched an eyebrow as we turned off the highway onto a service road. The undulating hills soon flattened as we turned toward the coast once more. We came about a bend near a rugged cliffside and the ocean came into view, blue and white with crawling breakers.

"It's lovely," she sighed. "Though not as pretty as the Pacific Ocean. Have you ever been to Cali, Wolf?"

"A couple of times, on business. Never made it out to the beach." I turned toward her with my lips thoughtfully pursed. "And you know my real name now, so you don't have to call me Wolf."

"Yeah, I don't *have* to." Scarlett gave me a teasing smile. "Of course, I'm still your captive, so I have to do whatever you say, call you whatever you want…"

The strap of her sun dress slid down her arm, and she made no move to replace it even though a vast expanse of freckled cleavage was exposed. I swallowed hard while my cock grew equally so.

"In that case, you can call me Daddy," I growled low. I'd intended to be flip, but as soon as the words left my mouth, I remembered that Scarlett had daddy issues in spades.

"Oh, okay, if you say so… *Daddy*." She released a girlish giggle. Scarlett twirled her hair around her finger, and then suddenly dropped a hand right onto my ever-hardening rod, massaging it through my pants.

"Do you want me to crash the car?" The smile on my face belied the harshness of my tone.

"Surely a big, strong man like my Daddy can handle a little H-job without being too distracted?" she teased, massaging me more firmly. My teeth clenched, and a low growl escaped my throat, which only seemed to encourage her.

We were only saved from imminent catastrophe by our prompt arrival at the nondescript fog-shrouded docks. A moderate gaggle of boating enthusiasts flitted about as they prepared to take advantage of the first decent weather in days. The sea might have been a bit choppy, but that wasn't about to dampen their enthusiasm—pun thoroughly intended.

All the people made me less nervous, not more, since Scarlett and I were less likely to be remembered. Between her hat and glasses-shrouded features, and the fact the media outlets had yet to mention any disappearance, I felt confident we'd be able to remain incognito.

It seemed a few gawkers and eyewitnesses were the only thing to be concerned about. I had begun to grow wary of how the entire snatch and grab had gone down thus far. Hunter Shaw hemming and hawing about paying the ransom, the way Devlin kept messing with me in subtle ways, like not stocking the safe house, and my unexpected and ferocious attraction to Scarlett made this far from a routine gig.

"Keep your hat on." I removed her hand from my crotch, albeit with more than a little reluctance. "Don't talk to anyone. Just keep walking."

"I feel like I'm in a spy movie," Scarlett chuckled.

I glanced at her sharply, my tone growing rough. "This isn't a movie, Red. Something is going on here that doesn't feel right, and it's got me on edge. I've learned to trust these feelings of mine, so please, just do as I say. Okay?"

"Okay, Will," she said, holding up a restraining palm. "I understand how important this is to you."

"Not just to me, to both of us." Then I had to look away because I couldn't fathom what was happening in my chest when I gazed into her green eyes.

I extracted the suitcase from the back, which I'd packed with a few clothing changes and basic toiletries. We weren't going to be out at sea for more than a day or two, or so I hoped. Scarlett arched a crimson brow at the sight of it, and I realized it was the same case I'd packed her into at the rave.

Her gaze rose to mine, narrowed and a little bit miffed. I shrugged slightly, as if to say, "What could I have done differently?" and she relaxed.

I moved around the car and onto the sun-warmed wooden planks of the dock, the wheels of the case clicking as we passed each timber. Scarlett rushed to catch up and entangled her arm into my own.

"We're trying to blend, remember?" She smiled and I smiled back because having her curvy little body next to mine felt fantastic. My mind began to race with possibilities of how we would pass the time on the open ocean...

We passed some nice-looking craft of different varieties, their only common feature that they were play toys of the well-off. Sailing skiffs, speed pleasure boats, and medium-sized yachts bobbed in the moderately choppy sea, each with a name that the owners probably thought a lot cleverer than they actually were.

But all of them paled in comparison to the sleek, dual-decked luxury craft moored at the end of the docks. Streamlined from bow to stern, the modern yacht wasn't overly large, but it more than made up for its size with what lurked under the gleaming skin.

"Wow..." Scarlett's mouth fell open as she scanned her sunglass-shrouded gaze over the yacht. "First you berate me for saying this is like a spy movie, and then you show me your boat, which is straight out of James Bond." She turned and punched me playfully in the deltoid. "Just saying," she giggled.

"I didn't custom order her," I replied wryly. "I won her in a poker game."

"No shit?" Scarlett shook her crimson tresses. "This just gets better and better."

She adopted a gruff tone and puffed out her chest. It took me a second to realize it was an imitation of me. "This isn't a game, baby girl," she seethed through clenched teeth. I didn't think that I sounded like that, but maybe I did. It sort of made me self-conscious. "Everything is *dead serious* and if you give me any lip, I'll shove a ball gag in your mouth and tie you to a chair."

I winced as her loud portrayal drew attention from the other boating enthusiasts.

"Shh, not so loud." I leaned in close as if I were simply giving her a hug. "Which brings me to my next order of business. If you want to leave and go back to your father, now is the time."

She recoiled from my touch, her mouth flying open and bottom lip trembling as she gaped up at me. "You—you want me to leave?" Hurt filled every word.

"What?" I grimaced. Why do women always have to take things the wrong way? "No, of course not. I'm just saying that this is your last chance to walk away from this mess. I'm sure your father would be happy to see you safe and sound."

"You're sure," she drawled the words, shaking her head. "You are. I'm not so certain about that, Will. If you're giving me a choice, I'm choosing to stay with you until this is over."

That was the answer I hoped for, desperately, the one I wanted to hear the most. But my conscience wouldn't let things just lie there.

"Think carefully, Red," my tone grim. "My family, the people we do jobs for… we're not the guys in white hats. We don't ride into town at the last minute to save it from the outlaws. A lot of times, we're working for the outlaws, even if it's only after the fact. If you stay, you might get the same taint that follows me around."

She laughed, a bitter sound that made me flinch from the weight of her grief. "Our families aren't as dissimilar as you seem to think they are, Big Bad Wolf." She put her foot on the extendable gangplank. "In all the world, you're the only one who's ever promised I won't get hurt."

"Your father never said anything like that to you?" I frowned. Not that my father had, either, but I recognized that a parent was supposed to say things like that.

"No." She was halfway up the gangplank at that point. "Are you coming or not? I can't exactly tie myself to a chair, you know."

I laughed as I walked up behind her. My voice and gaze were warm when I spoke. "We're past the point of tying you to chairs, Scarlett."

"Oh, well, that's too bad." She turned her back on me to walk up the gangplank. She gave her ass so much extra wiggle in the process that I had no choice but to smack it firmly with my hand, spurring her to greater speed.

Once on board, I showed her around. The yacht wasn't huge, but it featured a kitchen, shower, and lounge area, which could be opened up to the fishing deck at the stern. Needless to say, everything was impeccably chic and modern, as well as comfortable.

It had a bedroom, which I hoped to show her as well, but she stopped next to the fishing rig.

"This looks like serious business," she whistled. "My dad had a rig like this one, with the swivel chair and everything, but he never used it much."

"Are you into fishing?"

"Yeah, as long as I'm using a lure and not live bait. I know, hypocritical to kill the fish but not the worm."

"No, I think I get it," I replied.

I showed her how to work the rod, seeing the strain on her slender shoulders as she struggled to cast. Then I left her to it while I piloted us out into the open ocean. It was a bit choppy, with two-foot swells, but the yacht glided over them with ease so long as I went slowly enough.

When we were a couple of miles from shore, Scarlett's shout brought me running back down to the lower deck, but then I found that there was no emergency other than a severely bent rod and a flabbergasted redheaded heiress trying to keep an Atlantic cod from dragging her into the water.

I took over reeling it in and congratulated her on hooking the whopping forty-pounder.

"Looks like you've taken care of dinner, Red," I grinned.

"Mmm," she slipped her arm around my waist and pressed those wonderful breasts into my rib cage. "So long as you're taking care of… dessert."

Chapter Sixteen

Scarlett

IT WAS HARD TO BELIEVE IT, BUT I FELT AT PEACE.

With my legs dangling over the edge of the yacht, the waves gently lapping at the hull, I experienced a sense of tranquility I hadn't faced in a long time. Some would think being kidnapped and manhandled by my Big Bad Wolf would drive a girl to madness, but that wasn't what happened. In fact, it was just the opposite.

"Don't fall," Will called from behind me, and I glanced at him over one shoulder.

Smiling, I pushed myself up to my feet, my body lazy and sluggish. It couldn't be any other way—after such a good meal, one we had captured, gutted, and cooked ourselves—my belly was full, and I was content. Besides, it didn't hurt that I was spending the night on a yacht.

Yeah, I liked yachts. What kind of girl didn't? Especially when the only man on board was a handsome Wolf.

"You'd catch me before I could fall."

"Would I?" He cocked one eyebrow up and crossed his arms over his chest. Frowning, I kicked him in the ankle as hard as I could. He didn't move an inch, but I felt lightning shoot up my leg. "No strength, huh? Maybe you should give up on the yoga and start lifting weights."

"And become a mountain of muscles like you?" I threw back at him although I smiled now. Whenever he stood close to me, I simply couldn't help myself. "No, thank you. I'd rather remain my pretty self… and I think you prefer it, too."

"Is that so?"

"What are you doing?" I laughed. "Playing hard to get?"

As if to prove a point, I waltzed toward him.

I went on tiptoes and brushed my lips against his, my eyelids fluttering as his manly scent hit me. I placed my hands on his chest, my fingers above his beating heart, and felt a pleasant warmth spread all over my body. The memories of what we had done in the beach house hit me at once, and my nipples became hardened within the confines of my bra. My nipples weren't the only part of me reacting to those memories. I felt myself become wet, the fabric of my thong sticking to my skin as it absorbed my own juices. I just wanted to tease him, but I figured I'd ended up teasing myself.

"You want to head into the cabin?" I whispered, my fingers now wandering over the patch of naked skin between his shirt and pants. I felt the hard groove of his abs, the warmth of his skin, and it took all of my willpower not to go for his cock. As much as I wanted to, I didn't rush things.

"Why?" A grin spread across his lips. "Here's more than fine." Laying both hands on my ass, his large palms cupping my backside, he pulled me against him. Through the layers of our clothing, I felt the massive shape of his cock throbbing against my hip, and I became even wetter, so much that dehydration became a real concern.

"Here's fine," I repeated, fully knowing he always got his way. I didn't mind. From what I had experienced before, his way usually ended up with me coming so hard my brain melted inside my skull. No complaints there.

Kissing me deeply, he parted my lips with the tip of his tongue, one of his hands now resting on the nape of my neck. As for the other, his long fingers reached for the warmth between my legs. He flattened his palm against my mound, pressing down on my pussy, and a soft little moan escaped from my lips.

He didn't bother with teasing me.

He retreated and gathered the fabric of my dress, hand disappearing beneath the cloth. He slid his fingers in, moving them past my thong's elastic band. Trembling under his touch, his fingers brushed against my clit and inner lips, and I closed my eyes as the entire world seemed to fade. It seemed as if nothing but our bodies existed in the universe, and that suited me just fine.

"I love how wet you get." His voice came at me as if he stood on the other side of the universe. I was so out of it. My mind spun, and I felt all of my brain's processing power was hogged by the way his fingers moved against my pussy. To say this about any other man would have been a lie, but Will was impossibly good. So much that he should be outlawed. "And you're so fucking tight."

With that, he slipped a finger inside me, turning it around as he massaged my inner walls. At the same time, he placed his thumb over my clit and didn't waste a second. He stroked it right away, his finger moving in maddening circles around the bundle of nerves, and a column of fire rose up the length of my spine.

"That feels so good," I muttered, my heart pounding. My nipples became even harder, so much that the cups of my bra felt like an uncomfortable nuisance. As if he could read my mind, the hand he had on my neck fell, and he took my shirt off with a quick movement. Just as quickly, his fingers returned to my back, and he undid the clasp of my bra with a quick flick. The cups drooped over my breasts and, as he tore the bra off of me, my breasts spilled free.

All the while, the hand in my pants never stopped.

"It should be illegal for anyone to look this good, Scarlett," he breathed out, his eyes taking in every detail of my naked breasts. With just one finger, he traced their contour, his fingertip navigating around their base before marching up to my left nipple. He pinched it between his thumb and index finger, and I opened my mouth to let out a silent scream.

As he squeezed my nipple even harder, the pain turned into pleasure by the time it reached my brain. That's when he pushed another finger deep inside me. Turning his hand around, he massaged my pussy with maddening patience, and I couldn't stop myself from thinking he prepared my body for his massive cock. Judging by what had happened last time, I didn't think I needed a warm-up, but I wasn't going to stop him either. After all, this was *exactly* the kind of warm-up I loved.

"Fuck," I groaned, my eyes rolling as he pushed a third finger inside me. Flicking his wrist, he tore into my pussy hard, his hand trapped by my clothing.

"Fuck?" he repeated, that maddening grin of his returning. "That comes later." With that, he leaned in and sucked my free nipple into his mouth, his teeth gently grazing the nub. He whipped at it with his tongue, doing it in an almost violent manner, and pleasure spread its wings inside me. It didn't take long before my whole body trembled, my muscles turning into a gelatinous mass. From there it was only a matter of seconds until I came undone.

My pussy tightened around his fingers, forcing him to slow, and I felt the crack of a whip against my mind as I exploded. Now, more than just my pussy succumbed to spasms. My whole body seemed to shake and tremble, almost as if someone had tased me.

Moaning, I tilted my head back and stared up at the darkened sky, a billion stars sprinkled all over that dark blanket. It was the perfect scenery and, somehow, it made me feel emotional. Had anyone told me that I would be kidnapped by a brute like my Big Bad Wolf, and that he'd make me come like no one had ever done before, I'd have just laughed. To be kidnapped would be unbelievable enough, not to mention that there was no chance I'd let a hardened criminal lay his hands on me. Or so I thought. How things changed.

"That was incredible," I muttered, my body trembling as he slid his fingers out from my drenched pussy. Before I even knew what I was doing, I grabbed him by the wrist. I brought his hand up and forced him to brush his wet fingers over my lips. My inner voice screamed at me, *Have you lost your fucking mind, Scarlett?* But I just ignored it. It felt good to be wild.

Closing my eyes, I opened my mouth and allowed him to slip his fingers past my lips. I ran my tongue between his fingers, sucking them dry, and my heart tightened as I realized I tasted myself. I still wasn't sure about how he did it, but there was no denying it—whenever we were together like this, I just fucking lost my mind. Something inside me snapped whenever his hands were on me, and I just chucked all decency out the window.

"You're good with your mouth," he whispered softly, his fingers moving in and out at a gentle rhythm.

"Oh, you have no idea," I threw at him, rolling my lips back. His fingers popped out of my mouth with a wet sound and, before my inner voice could protest, my knees buckled under my weight. The moment they touched the deck, a wild smile dawned on my lips, the contour of his massive cock against his jeans enough to silence whatever rationality still lived inside me.

I reached for him like a wild animal, tearing his belt out as if I didn't have more than five minutes to live. I yanked his pants down, my hands turning into desperate claws, and his boxer briefs followed shortly after. His cock sprang free, slapping me across the back of my hand, and my pupils dilated as I took in his size. I had felt how large he was before, but I had never seen his cock up close.

Slowly, I reached for it and laid my fingers on his flesh. I gripped him by the root, his cock throbbing against the palm of my hand, and started moving my fingers up and down his length. I did it with a smooth coming and going motion, one that was almost hypnotizing, and I leaned into him even before I knew that I was doing it.

My lips parted of their own accord, and I closed my eyes as my tongue escaped from between them. The moment it touched the tip of his cock, the saltiness of his pre-cum coated my tongue, and I couldn't resist the urge to go one step further. Opening my mouth as wide as I could, I allowed him inside and wrapped my lips around his hard member. I kept on going, slowly pushing my mouth down, and only stopped when I felt him pressed against the back of my throat.

"Good girl." He laid both hands on my head. He threaded his fingers into my hair, held my head in place for a couple of heartbeats, and then dictated my movements. Surrendering all my free will, I bobbed my head, the pace increasing with each passing second.

It didn't take long before I gave him all that I had, the wet sound of my lips rolling up and down his cock blending with that of the waves lapping at the yacht. Cupping his balls with one hand, I used the other to match the motion of my mouth, and I stroked him with the same intensity with which I sucked and licked.

Before I met him, I thought going down on a man was something you did to pleasure *him*. Now, I finally understood I was looking at it the wrong way. Or maybe, I had just never met a man who made me experience things in such a way. Against all odds, I enjoyed sucking him even more than he did, and I wouldn't have minded spending the rest of my night there, down on my knees as he fucked my little mouth.

"So fucking good," he growled, his fingers tightening against my scalp. He put a stop to my pendulum motion and, taking control, he rocked his hips. I felt his flesh sliding back and forth, the warmth of it driving me completely crazy, and a wicked moan rose up my throat.

Suddenly, his cock throbbed against my tongue, weighing it down, and I wondered if he had reached his limit. Cupping my own breasts, my hard nipples trapped under my fingers, I readied myself to have him explode inside my mouth, but he seemed to have other plans. He pulled back from me, his cock popping out of my mouth, and then took me by the hand. He tugged on it, wanting me to stand up, but I didn't.

Instead, I just grinned.

"No," I told him, and surprise flashed across his eyes. He wasn't the kind of man who was used to hearing no, and I didn't think he had ever relinquished control when it came to sex. Hell, I didn't think, up until that moment, he had relinquished control when it came to *anything*. "You come here," I continued, and grabbing his wrist with both my hands, I pulled him down.

He knelt in front of me, a blend of confusion and anticipation washing over his face. Moving fast, I placed both hands on his chest and pushed him down until he lay on the deck, and that's when I climbed on top of him. Digging my fingertips into his chest, hard enough to draw blood, I leaned down until our lips were no more than a single inch apart.

"Now it's my turn," I whispered.

"Your turn for what?"

I didn't answer his question.

At least not with words.

Chapter Seventeen

Will

I HAD NEVER MET ANYONE LIKE HER.

She was fire and ice, sanity and madness. She was everything I never knew I wanted, a fragile and delicate thing that was mine to break and corrupt. Thing was, right now it looked like she was the one about to do the breaking and corrupting. Her innocent looks had given way to a wild expression, and blue flames of lust danced in her eyes. I might have been the Big Bad Wolf, but she had the look of someone with a leash in her hands.

Straddling me, her knees on either side of my thighs, she moved her fingers down my stomach. Slowly, she reached for my cock, gripping it so tightly that I couldn't stop myself from groaning. It seemed like she had taken a liking to the art of pain. This could be fun.

"How does it feel to not be in control?" she whispered, her narrowed eyes locked on mine. As she spoke, she raised her hips slightly, creating an opening between our bodies. She used that opening to angle my cock down and, taking complete control of what was happening, she started massaging her own pussy with the tip of my hardness. My body reacted on pure instinct and I thrust upward, but she was quick to put a stop to it.

Slamming the open palm of her free hand on my chest, she forced me to remain still, her smile widening into a grin.

"Don't even think about it." She continued to move the tip of my cock over the length of her inner lips. She teased me, driving me crazy, and she loved every fucking second. "I'm in charge now."

"You're only in charge because I *let* you be in charge," I told her, and she answered that by tightening her fingers around my cock even more. "Fuck," I breathed out, my thoughts turning into ash inside my head.

I'm a pretty wild guy when it comes to fucking a woman's brains out, but I had never had anyone make me feel like that. My mind was completely blank, and the concepts of past and future seemed to be nothing but stupid inventions. Right then, I was fully in the present. I had fucking transcended everything and achieved enlightenment, all because she gripped my cock.

"I know what you want," she continued, slowly allowing a single inch of my cock inside her pussy. My flesh throbbed violently against her fingers, the wet warmth of her pussy almost making me come. It took every ounce of self-restraint that I had to stop it from happening. "You want to fuck me. Don't you? You want to slide this hard cock of yours deep inside me. Don't you?"

"You have no idea how hard I'm going to fuck you, Scarlett," I growled, and I meant it. Shit, I had never meant anything as much as that. By the time I was done with her, she wouldn't even be capable of recalling her own name.

Bending over, her hair cascading over my chest, she tugged on my bottom lip with her teeth. She ran the tip of her tongue over the gap between my lips, and then laid maddening kisses on my neck. Then, her tongue circled back to my mouth, and she only stopped when her lips were pressed against my ear.

"I'm counting on it," she whispered, her voice slipping into my brain and choking whatever common sense I still had. "But first, I'm going to give you a taste of what I can do."

She did it fast and mercilessly.

She slammed herself down on my cock, my full length piercing her in a fraction of a second. Her mouth hung open, her eyes becoming as wide as plates, and her inner walls became so tight around my cock it almost seemed she wanted to choke it out.

"I love how hard you are," she swayed her hips as she annihilated me completely. Rocking her body with furious movements, her body undulating like a whip cutting through the air, she did what she had promised and gave me a taste of what she was capable of. And what she was capable of... holy fuck, it was heaven on Earth.

"I love how fucking dirty you can be." I brought my hands down on her ass with a quick movement, slapping her flesh, and the sound of it exploded into the air. Digging my fingers into her ass cheeks, I surrendered to the violent motion of her body, and only then did I realize just how close I was to coming. I took one deep breath, my whole body tensing, and did my best to stop it from happening.

It was useless.

For the first time in my life, I had lost control of my body, and my cock thrashed inside her viciously. Thrusting upward, so fast and hard that her knees left the ground for a second, I shot all my seed inside her. I gritted my teeth so hard that pain shot up my jaw, and a thermonuclear detonation went off inside my head, obliterating everything I was.

I know I said I'd make her forget her own name, but it seemed like she had done it to me first. What was my name? I didn't have a fucking clue, and I couldn't give any less of a shit. I was experiencing the highest high of my entire fucking life, and that was the only thing that truly mattered. It might sound like an exaggeration, but had I died that very second, I would have died a truly happy man.

"That was amazing," she whispered softly, the frantic motion of her body finally ceasing. My eyes snapped open as I heard her words, and I found a rush of adrenaline coursing through my veins.

"*Was amazing?*" I repeated, and I suddenly felt the urge to laugh. I didn't. Instead, I brought one hand up to her throat and tightened my fingers around her neck. "Scarlett, I'm only getting started." Before she could say a thing, I pushed my hips up and rolled to the side. I forced her down onto the deck, switching positions with her, and she wrapped her legs around my waist.

I started thrusting right away.

My cum and her juices acted as a lubricant, and my cock slid in so damn easily that it was hard to believe this was actually happening. I was no longer thinking about what I was doing, nor was I simply going through the motions. My mind, body, and soul had become one, and they had coalesced around a single and bright purpose—to fuck Scarlett as intensely as I could.

"Harder," she screamed, her voice carried away by the ocean breeze. "Harder."

I was more than happy to oblige.

Sliding out from inside of her, I was about to turn her around when she sprang up. Before I could do a damn thing about it, she sat up on the deck and dove forward with her open mouth. Her lips rolled down my cock in a flash, and I threw my head back as I felt her tongue dancing around its tip. She moaned softly, cleaning my cock with the smooth strokes of her tongue, and she only pulled back once she was satisfied.

"You're fucking amazing," I told her and finally reached for her again. Hooking my fingers on the back of her knees, I dragged her toward me and forced her to turn around. She didn't need any further instructions. She placed herself on all fours, wiggling her sweet little ass at me, and I closed the distance between us as fast as I could.

Grabbing my cock by the root, I pushed it down past her inner thighs and took a deep breath as I felt her inner lips around my tip once more. This time I took my time. I fed her one inch at a time, enjoying the way her moans kept getting louder and louder, and I only started going all out once I had sheathed my cock to the hilt. My thighs slapped her ass over and over again, the sound of flesh on flesh drowning her own moans, and I kept on doing it until we were nothing but two naked bodies trembling in ecstasy.

"Is this hard enough for you?" I growled, grabbing her hair and yanking on it. She threw her head back, her moans turning into a high-pitched scream, and I pistoned into her so hard she almost tipped forward. Holding onto her hair, I forced her to remain in place as I ravaged her, my cock slamming into her tight pussy without any mercy. "Or do you want me to go even harder?"

She didn't reply. Fuck, I didn't even know if she could hear me. She was so lost in her pleasure she seemed completely oblivious to everything around her. Thankfully, that was just the way I wanted her to be.

Grinning like a madman, I took my hands to her ass, and used my thumbs to caress the sweet space between her cheeks. With my heart pounding hard, I pressed one thumb against her back entrance and then eased it in. I felt her tense, her pussy tightening around my cock as her ass gripped my finger, and her body became as taut as a nocked arrow.

Before I could ready myself for it, she thrust back against me, impaling herself on my cock. She did it so suddenly I was caught by surprise, a violent burst of energy crashing down my spine and exploding up my cock.

"Holy fuck," I groaned, the spasms of her inner walls massaging my cock. I came for the second time in a row and, as unbelievable as it may seem, I filled her pussy up even more than I had the first time. My cock kept throbbing for what seemed like an eternity and, when I finally looked down, I saw thick ropes of semen dripping out from her pussy and down her thighs. The sight of it was mesmerizing.

One deep breath and she finally tipped forward.

She collapsed on the wooden deck, limbs sprawled to the side. Her hair fell around her head like a luscious crown, and I watched her back moving softly as she tried to catch her breath. Used and spent, she had never looked so beautiful. Had I ever met a woman this amazing? One capable of making my heart skip a beat and turning my cock into a tireless sledgehammer? No, *never*. And that was because Scarlett was one of a kind.

Careful now, I thought, *you're playing a dangerous game.*

"Yeah," I muttered under my breath. "And I'm fucking lovin' it."

Chapter Eighteen
================

Will

Scarlett slept.

Lying next to her, the gentle sway of the boat rocking us, I was at peace. Almost as if nothing outside of this cabin mattered. My family became nothing but an unimportant detail in the grand scheme, and the same was true of her father. I knew the real world waited for us, somewhere past the blue surface of the ocean, but I tried to keep it at bay. I didn't want reality to ruin this moment.

Outside, the sun had nearly completed its lazy descent toward the horizon line, the brightness of the day slowly turning into a mellow orange glow. We had spent most of the night awake—our bodies had demanded it—and that resulted in us spending the day in bed. I had never been the kind of guy to be idle, especially during a job, but it wasn't exactly like I had a lot to do. This was a waiting game, after all.

Of course, Scarlett made it easy to wait. Her body had kept me busy all night long and, against all odds, I found it comfortable to be around her. It wasn't just sexual either. I didn't exactly know what it was about her, but it felt right to be sharing a bed with her, talking about nothing and everything until we both drifted off to sleep, and—

"Get ahold of yourself," I muttered under my breath, mentally slapping myself. I knew the last thing a person should do during a kidnapping job was get attached to the subject, and so I had to keep my head on my shoulders. Of course, it was already a bit too late. I did my best to ignore it, but the fact was that I cared about Scarlett. Why else would I have left the beach house and brought her to the yacht? "You're a fucking idiot, Will."

"No guns," Scarlett mumbled in her sleep, stirring softly. She balled one hand into a fist, waved it around as if she were a drunk protestor, and then rolled to the side of the bed, tangling her legs in the sheet. "Say no to guns." She didn't open her eyes as she spoke, and soon enough she fell silent again, her chest rising and falling at a gentle pace.

Shaking my head, I swung my legs out of the bed.

I grabbed my pants from the floor, got inside of them, and then slipped out of the cabin. The ocean remained calm, its surface reflecting the setting sun. There wasn't a single cloud in the sky but, just to make sure, I headed into the pilot house to check the weather reports. The last thing we needed was to find ourselves in the middle of a storm and, even if that seemed unlikely, I wanted to make sure.

Sinking into the pilot's chair, I confirmed the weather wouldn't go crazy on us and then made a quick check of the instruments. We had enough fuel to last us for weeks, especially considering the yacht simply idled in its current position, and the radar wasn't picking up any boats in the vicinity. As it was, we were perfectly removed from the world. For the time being, Scarlett was safe.

"For the time being," I said out loud, lips pursed tight. Devlin's instructions had been clear. Unless Scarlett's father paid up, I was to get rid of her. I clenched my jaw as I imagined a scenario in which that would happen, and quickly realized I simply *couldn't* picture the event. There was no way I'd be able to kill her. Fuck Devlin and his stupid instructions. If the family wanted Scarlett, they'd have to deal with me first.

Raking one hand over my face, I pushed myself up to my feet and then started rummaging through the cabinets at the back of the room. Once I found what I was looking for—a half-empty bottle of Macallan '18—I poured two fingers of it into a lowball glass. It was bad form to drink during a job, especially if that meant doing it while at the helm of a yacht, but I didn't care. This whole thing was fucked.

Suddenly, I felt the burner phone vibrate against my leg. I fished it from my pocket and frowned as I recognized Devlin's number on the screen. Not that I was surprised. After all, no one else had this number.

Frowning, phone in one hand and whiskey in the other, I wandered out of the pilot house and onto the prow. For a moment, I considered not picking up and even imagined myself throwing the phone into the ocean. It was highly unlikely Devlin would have good news for me, and I wasn't exactly in the mood to put up with his bullshit. Still, it had to be done.

"What?" I pressed the phone against my ear.

"We have a problem," Devlin confirmed my suspicions. Then and there, I regretted not throwing the phone into the sea when I had the chance. When had Devlin ever been the bearer of good news? The man was a walking bad omen and always seemed happy about it. "The girl's father isn't getting the message. He probably doesn't think we're serious."

"And how's that my problem?" I threw back at him, my fingers tightening around the phone so much I heard its plastic case creak. "Convince him we're serious. That's your job, not mine."

"Wow, that's genius," he laughed, and I pictured my fist flying straight to his face. Man, wouldn't that be grand. "I hadn't thought of it, Will. Seriously, that was pure brilliance. I'm going to call him right now and tell him that we're big boys and should be taken seriously. He'll be shaking in his boots, huh?"

"Cut the shit, Devlin," I growled. "You're not as funny as you think you are."

"And here I was, thinking I was hilarious." He released a faux sigh and then cleared his throat. "Seriously, though. Her father is acting all wishy-washy, and it doesn't look like he's willing to pay the ransom. The asshole probably thinks we won't do anything to his girl and we'll just let her go eventually."

"But we will let her go."

"If he pays up, yeah," Devlin continued. "The problem is he isn't paying. It's an annoyance, but I think we have to send him some proof that we're serious."

"Proof?" I repeated, even though I was pretty sure what was coming. Most rich assholes had a hard time parting with their money but, more often than not, a finger or an ear helped them remember their bank account's information. My stomach lurched as I imagined a sharp blade cutting through Scarlett's tender skin, and I gritted my teeth so hard pain shot up my jaw. "It's still early in the game, Devlin. We need to be patient. Once he realizes his daughter won't be returning anytime soon, then he'll—"

"Since when did you become a gambler, Will?" he cut me short. "I'm not here to gamble. I'm here to rig the table, turn the odds in our favor, and make a shitload of money. That's how we operate. Remember? Or have you forgotten just who your family is?"

"Fuck you."

"Yeah, well." Even though I couldn't see him, I knew he shrugged in that casual manner of his. "How soon can you send me one of her toes? I don't want you mailing it directly to the guy."

"A toe?"

"What? You think an ear would be better?" He was clearly oblivious to the anger in my voice. "No, I don't think so. I've seen pictures of her, and I wouldn't want to ruin that pretty little face. It might piss the old man off, and I don't want him digging in his heels even more than he has already. Although, if he insists on not paying, I figure an ear might help him realize how committed we are. For now, though, a toe will suffice. Just remember to pack it in ice, so that—"

"I'm not going to chop off one of her fucking toes." Still holding the glass of whiskey, I felt the urge to smash it against Devlin's face. If only the asshole wasn't a thousand miles away. "I promised her she wouldn't be hurt and—"

"And why the fuck would you promise her that?" He sounded genuinely baffled. "You're not running a daycare there, Will. This is a fucking op, not a dating reality show. Jesus, man. Now, listen, how fast can you get me that toe? I'm starting to get impatient and—"

"I told you already," I spoke through gritted teeth. "I'm not going to do that."

"Oh, but you will. Because if you don't, I will be forced to take measures."

"Devlin?"

"Yeah?"

"Fuck you." I slammed my thumb against the phone's screen, terminating the call. For a moment, I considered just throwing the damn thing overboard. Instead, I pushed the phone back in my pocket and drank the rest of my whiskey in a single gulp. The alcohol burned its way down my throat, viciously clawing at my insides, and I let out an exhausted groan.

"This is fucking bullshit," I muttered, cocking my arm back and throwing the lowball glass at the ocean. It flew up into an arch before disappearing with a barely audible *plop*. I knew I shouldn't have accepted the job. This had never been my kind of gig.

Sure, I'd chopped off my fair share of toes, thumbs, and ears, and I never let anything stop me from finishing a mission, but now... I simply couldn't bring myself to do it. There was no way I was going to hurt Scarlett, even if that meant I was fucking up the operation.

You're in too deep now, I thought, coming to terms with everything that had happened. Ever since that first time together, I had stopped giving a shit about the mission. Sure, I wouldn't mind seeing it through, just as long as that meant I'd be able to return Scarlett to her life, safe and unharmed. As that seemed more unlikely, though, my priorities shifted.

In the end, it was clear what was happening. Against my best judgement, I had started caring for her. Just two weeks ago, I would've laughed at such a stupid thing. I wasn't in the habit of *caring* about anyone, and that was even truer if we were talking about a target. Somewhere down the road, though, Scarlett had stopped being a target. She was just... *Scarlett.*

Leaning against the railings, I turned around as I heard a sound coming from inside the cabin. Scarlett was up. Had she heard my conversation with Devlin? If she had, there was no way I'd be able to hide how serious things were getting.

Fuck, what a shitstorm.

Chapter Nineteen

Scarlett

"Will?" I sat on the bed and stifled a yawn as I looked around the cabin.

I was still naked, the bedsheet bunched up around my waist, but I didn't bother covering myself. After all, Will had already seen every inch of my naked body. It was too late to play coy now, not to mention I enjoyed the way he couldn't help himself around my nakedness.

Stretching my back, I looked around the cabin, but Will was nowhere to be seen. I got up, grabbed my clothes from the floor, and got dressed. My hair was a disheveled mess, and even though I tried to finger-comb the strands, it didn't help much. The saltiness in the air made it curly and wild, and I knew I needed a long shower before I'd be able to tame my mane.

I padded my way toward the door but, when I heard voices outside, I froze. Will was out on the deck, and he spoke with someone. Had someone from his organization landed on the yacht while I slept? He didn't tell me he was waiting for anyone, so what the hell was going on?

Quietly, I pressed my ear against the door, and only then did I realize the only voice I heard was Will's. He had to be talking on the phone. I was about to open the door and step outside when he raised his voice, and his words gave me pause.

"I'm not going to chop off one of her fucking toes." It felt as if someone had punched me in the gut. "I promised her she wouldn't be hurt and—"

Holy shit. That didn't sound good.

Instinctively, I looked down at my feet and wiggled my toes. I couldn't imagine my father being happy about receiving a toe in the mail, but I didn't believe it would convince him to fork over the money either. Hell, they could mail him an entire foot, and I doubt that'd make a difference.

Slowly, I pushed the door open and I stepped outside. Will leaned against the railings, his hair gently ruffled by the sea breeze. The creases on his forehead had deepened into hard lines. He tried smiling when he noticed me leaving the cabin, but I could tell he was just trying to put on a mask. Whatever conversation he had been having, it hadn't gone well. Then again, a conversation that involved plans to mail toes was bound to leave anyone in a foul mood.

"So," I started. "Which of my toes are you going to cut off?"

"You heard."

"I did." Nodding, I headed toward him. I placed my hands on the railings, the hem of my dress flapping in the wind, and allowed my eyes to be drawn by the ocean's calm surface. "I heard you say you wouldn't do it, so thank you."

"No need to thank me," he grumbled. "I'm not in the habit of going around chopping people up." He paused, almost as if he remembered that his job involved exactly that. "I mean, it's not my favorite thing in the world."

"I assume my father's not cooperating?" I already knew the answer to that question. The asshole was probably drinking a celebratory whiskey and smoking a fat Cuban cigar, gleeful about the fact I had disappeared off the face of the earth. Sure, he did pay for most of my expenses—fair enough—but I knew it was only a matter of appearances. He wanted to position himself as an All-American do-gooder whose spoiled daughter had turned on him and, lo and behold, some publications had taken the bait.

"No, he hasn't paid yet," Will's voice was clipped. I could tell he struggled. "My associates believe we need to push him harder than we have, and that's why they wanted me to…"

"Cut off one of my toes. Right."

"Don't worry, though. I'm not gonna do that."

"Then what now?"

His lips turned into a thin, straight line. He looked away from me, his gaze locked on the horizon. Even though he didn't speak, I heard a hundred gears turning inside his head. Whatever the situation, it sure as hell wasn't good. So far, I had felt safe around him, but would that last? I had no idea what kind of influence Will wielded in his organization. If his associates wanted to kill me, would he be able to stop my death?

"I'm not sure," he finally spoke. "The family isn't that forgiving of those who break rank. I assume they might send someone to look for us."

"What for?" My stomach lurched as fear gripped me tightly. It was bad enough I had been kidnapped, but now it seemed like my situation was about to get worse.

"They'll probably want to assess my loyalty," Will replied. "If push comes to shove, they might even put a bullet between my eyes." He turned to look at me and, for the first time since I stepped onto the deck, he gave me a genuine smile. "Or, you know, they'll try. It's not like I'm going to make it easy."

"Would they really try to kill you?" My fingers tightened around the railing so much my knuckles turned white. I knew he cared for me, even if just a little, but I had never expected him to put his life on the line. Now, here he was, proclaiming he was more than willing to fight against his own association just to keep me safe. The world had been turned upside down. Up was down, down was up, and the Big Bad Wolf was now my rescuer. "That's insane. You've kidnapped me. You're doing what they want."

"The way they see it, I'm not trying hard enough."

"Jesus," I breathed out, suddenly feeling dizzy. Gritting my teeth, I gave myself an encouraging nod and turned to Will. "All right, you can cut off one of my toes. I won't be able to wear sandals ever again, but I'm willing to make the sacrifice."

"You—*what?*"

"You can cut off one of my toes," I repeated, trying to put as much steel and determination behind my voice as I could. I was actually surprised at how confident I sounded. In truth, I was scared shitless. I didn't even like needles, let alone knives or whatever these guys used to slice people up. "I don't want anyone to come after you, Will."

"You can't be serious." He shook his head and lowered his gaze. To his sides, his hands balled into fists. "I put you in this mess, and you'd still do something like that for me? Scarlett, I..." He trailed off, and his voice carried a gentle tone I wasn't used to. He was usually so brash and confident, and it threw me off balance to see him almost tamed. "Thank you, but no."

"I'm serious," I insisted. "I don't want you to get hurt."

"I'm not going to get hurt." Then he closed the distance between us. Laying one hand on my waist, he used the other to brush the hair away from my face. He smiled, and I smiled back. "If these fuckers try anything, they're going to regret it. This isn't my first rodeo, Scarlett. I can handle myself."

"Where does that leave us then?"

"I don't know." Then he leaned in and brushed his lips against mine. I closed my eyes, enjoying the way his lips felt when pressed to mine, and in that moment, everything was right with the world. "We'll figure it out, though. Whatever happens, no one's gonna touch a single hair on your head."

"Thank God for that," I laughed, "because my hair is shit right now. I don't want anyone to touch it." I placed one hand on his chest and looked into his eyes. I still didn't know how it had happened, but I felt safe around him. The man who had kidnapped me was the one who made me feel safe. If that wasn't ironic, I didn't know what was.

"I mean it," he whispered. "I don't care what I have to do, I'll make sure you're safe." He wet his lips and rocked softly on his heels, almost as if he was readying himself to say something. Then, when he finally spoke, his words hit me like a brick. "I love you, Scarlett. I really do. Whatever it takes to protect you, I will do it. I don't give a fuck if I have to go against my family, your father, or the entire fucking world… just as long as you're safe, I'm more than ready to beat them into a pulp."

For a moment, I said nothing.

I just stood there, looking at him as if I was seeing him for the first time in my life. I took in every line of his face, every angle of his chiseled jaw, and my heart tightened into the shape of a small coin. I knew that he cared for me, but *this*? To say I wasn't expecting it would put it mildly.

"I love you too," I found myself saying, the words slipping out from between my lips before I even knew what I'd said. It was true, though. Somehow, I had fallen in love with him. The Big Bad Wolf had turned into my protector, and my heart had opened up to let him in. Stepping forward, I fell into his embrace, laying my head on his chest as he wrapped his arms around me.

He laid one hand on the nape of my neck, cradling me against his chest, and soon enough we were kissing again. Our lips were like the two remaining pieces of a puzzle, and they clicked together so perfectly that—

"What's that?" Pulling back from him, I shaded my eyes from the sun with one hand. In the distance, backlit by the orange sun, a small dot seemed to be moving toward us. As the seconds passed, that dot acquired the contours of something resembling a small boat.

"Fuck," Will growled. "That's not good."

Chapter Twenty

Will

The red sun squatting low on the horizon splashed me and Scarlett with gentle light, belying our dire circumstances as I peered intently at the approaching boat.

"What do you see?" Scarlett prompted, looking to me with concern written over her freckled features.

"Trouble," I replied grimly. Dashing back inside the cabin, I retrieved a pair of binoculars residing in a magnetic case adhered to a metal support strut. Once back outside, I lifted them to my face and adjusted the focus with a practiced twitch of my index finger.

The boat resolved itself into an open-air single deck speeder. Probably a rental, judging from its worn glitter paint and the decal on the side featuring a crab in a life vest. Why would a crab need a life vest? But I digress.

Inside the boat were no less than seven men, maybe more, and they did not look like sportsmen out for a joyride. Hard expressions marred their already blunt and rugged features, haircuts at least a decade out of style, and a definite gritty edge.

Probably Russians, or Eastern Europeans, and definitely hired muscle. I could tell that even if I didn't see the AR-15 barrel jutting out from behind one man's shoulder.

I worried I'd made a mistake by moving us out of the safe house. Perhaps that's when they got onto our tail? But there was no way of knowing. It was equally possible that this team of scoundrels had stormed the beach house first, and then extrapolated our destination from there.

In any event, I thought of the snub nosed .38 revolver I carried in my pocket and realized it was no match for even a single AR-15-wielding thug. And there were far more than one.

"Get inside," I snapped at Scarlett. "Get low, as low as you can."

She looked from my grim face to the approaching boat and then rushed to obey. Scarlett plastered herself on the floor of the cabin, wedging herself between the metal wet bar and the kitchen console.

I dashed up to the pilot's compartment, taking the steps two at a time, and churned the engine to life. The yacht surged forward, spraying frothy water out the aft deck as our twin propellers twirled like whirling dervishes. I opened up the throttle all the way and angled our flight so we were taking the low Atlantic sea waves head on.

"Brace yourself, Scarlett!" I shouted over my shoulder as we hit the first raised hump of water. Though only a couple of feet, we hit the swell hard enough to take flight for a dozen feet, splashing back down and submerging the aft deck enough that the white sofa got wet.

Then it was on to the next wave, and the next, me just barely able to keep control of the yacht through the choppy seas. Every time we touched back down on the water, it was a struggle to keep her from fishtailing and spinning out.

Our yacht came equipped with lots of gadgets, including rear-facing cameras with a cockpit display. I spared a glance back at our pursuers while we were in a trough. My eyes narrowed as I realized they were, in fact, gaining upon us. They were now less than five hundred feet behind.

Their craft was lighter and gained more air on every jump. This didn't quite work to their advantage, however, since their pilot wasn't as used to his craft as I was to the yacht. I saw him frantically trying to turn the wheel and catch a rogue swell at the right angle, but we both knew he'd be too late.

I couldn't suppress a shout of triumph when the vessel hit the wave awkwardly and twisted slightly in the air. The boat splashed down hard, rocking the men inside of it before the propellers caught traction. Our pursuing boat skewed wildly to the side, tossing one of the men overboard with a terrified shout.

Watching carefully, I soon determined they were not going to stop and fish him out. Only one of the men even seemed concerned that they had a man overboard. This pissed me off because I put a high value on loyalty.

Not that I had been loyal enough to the firm to cut off one of Scarlett's toes, no matter how willing she may have been to go through with the torture. I swore no harm would come to her, and I damn sure meant the words.

Their error had cost them precious time, however. We gained nearly a thousand feet while their pilot recovered control of the boat. Yet regain control was what he did, and soon enough they gained on us once more.

The sun had just kissed the ocean, no longer quite a red circle in the sky as we passed a buoy declaring we were now in international waters. Not that I'd been expecting —or wanting—help from the authorities, but it was a grim reminder of how alone we really were. Those men could kill us with literally zero witnesses to tell the tale.

That whole saying about there being no God in international waters—it's not far from the mark. I checked the rear-facing camera monitor and found that they were less than three hundred feet away.

I did the calculations in my head. The AR-15 had a maximum effective range of four hundred meters, meaning they were well within rifle shot of our craft.

But most people couldn't fire accurately at more than fifty feet. That number dwindled the farther from your target you got. They weren't wasting their ammunition yet, but soon enough they'd be in range.

When I first enlisted, I was no stranger to guns. Unlike Scarlett, I never had a problem with firearms, and I figured I was in for no surprises in the armed forces. However, I was quite wrong. An AR-15's destructive power is a nightmare to behold. One of our drill instructors rigged up a pig carcass on a target as an analogue to show us what happens when it hits a human body.

That pig exploded into shredded meat and splintered bone, causing the most jaded of us to gape in horror. It was a hard lesson, deeply imbedded, and it was supposed to make us think twice before pulling the trigger because friendly fire isn't all that friendly, and does anyone really want to turn the ten-year-old Iraqi child throwing bricks at their position into shredded meat? Or did everyone want to accept the hit on their helmet and let him have a chance to grow up decent?

"Will!" Scarlett shouted over the din of our engines and the splashing waves. I turned my gaze just enough to spot her with my peripheral vision, standing behind my chair. Her hair was torn about in wild disarray by the wind, her dress billowing behind her. "They're getting closer."

"I told you to stay down," I growled, unable to do much about it at the time. I had to maintain control of the yacht.

"I can help you," she said.

"How?" I sputtered.

"There's a tank of propane next to the stove."

"And?" I blurted, struggling to keep us steady as we hit another swell.

"And..." She was jostled about on impact but managed to keep her footing. "And have you ever seen the movie *Jaws*?"

I hadn't, actually—judge me if you will, but I don't like effects films—but I knew enough about the finale to know what she was getting at.

"Take the wheel," I said, indicating the copilot's chair.

"But I've never..."

"Take the wheel, Scarlett," I snapped. There was no time to be polite. "Just keep the nose pointed at the oncoming waves."

She dropped into the seat, fearfully tightening her hands around the wheel. I leaped to my feet and dashed down the steps to the bottom deck. We impacted with another wave when I was halfway down, and I went sprawling onto my belly, cutting my lip when I hit the floor.

But I was back up immediately, rushing over to the secured propane tank and attacking the fastenings with fingers and thumbs. I grunted, struggling to remove the wingnuts, which had corroded stubbornly into place. My skin grew raw, my muscles cramped, but I refused to give in.

At last, I pried the fastenings free and skidded on my knees to the rear of the yacht. The boat full of hard-eyed men was less than a hundred feet away now. One of the AR-15-wielding men felt confident to aim a short burst in our direction. It harmlessly shot gouts of water up in our wake instead of striking our hull, but it was a clear reminder that soon we'd be sitting ducks for their potent arsenal.

"Du dunt du dunt du dunt, mother fuckers," I shouted, mimicking the famous theme song from the film. Then I heaved the propane tank over my head, preparing to launch it at our adversaries.

My plan was to toss it in their path and then draw my pistol and fire. Unfortunately, we hit the back side of a wave, and Scarlett's inexperienced hand cost us dearly. The yacht lurched badly to the left, sending me sprawling. I dropped the propane tank instead of a targeted throw, and it fell into our wake and was launched off into the deep harmlessly far away from our foes.

There was nothing to it. Scarlett couldn't handle the boat, not in these choppy waters, and we didn't stand a chance of winning a fire fight. I was going to have to engage the yacht's secret and hope the waves weren't too high for it to operate without us capsizing.

As I scrambled to my feet, more gunfire erupted from the pursuing boat. The white sofa erupted into gouts of stuffing as bullets tore it to shreds. I dashed up the steps as several splintered below me under the might of the assault rifles.

Running up to the top deck, I plopped heavily into the pilot's seat and took over the controls.

"I'm sorry, Will," Scarlett said, her eyes full of regret and fear.

"It's fine." I flipped open a metal caster on the control console. "We're about to leave these assholes far behind."

"What? Does this boat have hidden wings?" she snapped.

"In a manner of speaking, yes," I grinned. I pushed the button behind the caster. "I'm going to engage the hydrofoil mode. There's no way they'll be able to keep up with us."

I waited. Nothing happened. Gunfire tore into our aft deck as Scarlett turned a baleful eye my way.

"What's wrong?"

"I don't know," I snapped. "It's not working…"

My voice trailed off, and then I started cursing.

"Damn it, Will, what's the matter? Talk to me."

"The hydrofoils won't deploy because they're still locked in place for maintenance," I said. "They'll have to be manually released."

"Is that something you can do?" she said, fearfully watching the boat grow ever closer on the monitors.

"No," I said grimly. "It's something *you* have to do."

Scarlett's green eyes widened to the size of the setting sun.

"Me?"

Chapter Twenty-One

Scarlett

"What in the fuck did you just say?" My mouth gaped open. "I don't know anything about fixing boats."

"Do you know how to change a tire?" Wolf snapped back, his knuckles white on the wheel as gunfire rang out.

"Well, yes…"

"Then you can do this. It's much easier." Will's eyes narrowed. "Brace yourself."

I obeyed just in time as we hit a higher swell than we'd yet encountered. His expert handling meant we landed in a precisely aligned position and lost little momentum.

When our pursuers hit the same high swell, however, their pilot wasn't so skilled or lucky. The speed boat hit at an awkward angle and listed badly in the water. Will laughed triumphantly, though it was a momentary victory.

"Ha, they stalled out," he said with glee.

"Does that mean we're going to escape?" I asked. "And I don't have to fix the stupid boat?"

"Maybe, unless they get it going again quickly," he said, peering at the rear-mounted camera monitor. His eyes narrowed and he started cursing again. "Fuck. *Fuck.* They're already gaining on us again."

"Guess I have to fix the hydrofoil," I murmured with resignation. I ran my fingers over the edges of the control console, looking for a latch or release.

"What in the hell are you doing?" Will asked incredulously.

"I'm looking for a way to get this open. You said I had to fix the hydrofoil…" I glared at him hard. "We're being shot at and your stupid fancy boat is broken. Now is not the time to laugh."

"I'm sorry, babe," he said, gritting his teeth as we hit another wave. "But the console doesn't open, and that's not where the fastenings are."

"Then where are they?" I blurted, peering anxiously over my shoulder at the rapidly approaching boat. Unfortunately, it looked like their pilot had learned how to hit the swells more skillfully because they were no longer losing ground on impact.

"On the side of the boat, just above the water line," Will said.

"What?" I sputtered. "What am I supposed to do, cling to the side? Of a wet hull? On a moving boat? Who do you think I am, fucking Spider-Man?"

"I'd do it if I could, but I have to stay at the wheel." Will's tone was grim. "You can tie yourself off to the mooring rope and hang off the side."

I bit my tongue on an angry retort, thinking back to my teens when I went through a rock-climbing phase. That was before my father and I had a falling out, and he had eagerly paid for all my lessons and gear.

I thought perhaps Will's idea might be a valid one. If I tied the rope around my waist, and used it like I was rappelling… Yes, I could pull this off. Maybe.

"All right, Will." I tried to still my rapidly beating heart. "All right. I'll do it. I guess I have no choice. How do I unfasten the moorings?"

"There's an extra-large cotter key in that compartment," Will said, jutting his chin at a nearby console.

"What's a cotter key?" I snapped. "God, speak English. I don't know your nautical bullshit."

"It's not nautical—never mind. It looks like a bent bar as long as your forearm."

I stood up unsteadily on my feet and stumbled over to the cabinet in question. Flinging open the door, I spotted a ton of equipment, most of it secured to the cabinet wall with plastic ties. At first I was too frantic, too panicky, to discern any individual items.

But then another stream of deadly lead rain pattered onto our speeding boat, and I was pulled out of my fugue. I spotted what must have been the cotter key. It resembled a giant hairpin, with one end longer than the other. Unfortunately, it too was secured by zip ties.

Zip ties, handcuffs, duct tape—it seemed binding agents were the bane of my existence recently. I spied a sheathed survival knife hanging in the cabinet and yanked the blade free.

"Brace yourself," Will shouted, but it was too late for me to react. We impacted on the other side of a wave and I stumbled to the floor, the knife careening out of my grasp and sliding across the floor to tumble down to the lower deck.

"Goddamn it," I screamed, scrambling on all fours to the edge of the stairs. I clambered down carefully over the sundered steps while renewed gunfire rang out.

Wood splintered near my ear, causing me to shout and prostrate myself on the wooden deck. This put my hand within reach of the knife. I grabbed the handle and then raced back up the stairs, using the still-intact side.

"Where have you been?" Will demanded as I made it back to the cabinet.

"Ordering breakfast. Where the fuck do you think I've been?" I snapped. Either I was aggressive when scared, or Will had dragged a more swaggering side out of me. In either event, he shut up while I cut the cotter key free.

I almost wanted to laugh looking at it in my hand, because I realized at that moment this was the easy part of the operation. The easy part.

"Hang on, I'm going to hit this next wave at full speed and try to gain some distance on them," Will said.

We hit the surge hard, my teeth rattling together, but our landing was surprisingly smooth. We gained about fifty feet on our pursuers, which was still too close for comfort, but it was better than nothing.

I headed out onto the lower deck and quickly tied the mooring rope around my waist. By using the water line, I was able to accurately gauge how much slack I would need. Then I stepped up onto the edge of the safety railing and stared down at the green and white water rushing by below.

In that moment, I nearly lost my nerve. I could see the fastenings, and the rectangular slot where the cotter key was meant to go, but it seemed like suicide to try and engage it in the lock.

But then I remembered it wasn't just my life on the line. Will's was also at stake and he'd already risked so much for my sake. Maybe we didn't have a storybook beginning to our romance—God, it was the antithesis of a fairy tale, to be honest—but that didn't mean we couldn't have our happily ever after.

I steeled my nerves and then stepped over the railing, clinging to the rope with one hand. Muscle memory took over, and my bare feet adroitly slapped along the smooth hull as I rappel-walked along my tethered line.

Then I looked forward and growled in alarm. I grabbed the cotter key and hugged it to my body while clinging to the rope with both arms. We hit the swell, and I bounced painfully off the hull, nearly dropping the key.

But I held onto it, in spite of everything, and crawled out a little further. Straining my muscles and my sinews to the utmost limit, I managed to jam the end of the key inside the rectangular hole.

"Damn it," I growled. "Fucking turn. *Turn.*"

I felt the skin on my palm protest vehemently against the rough abrasion it suffered—I would wind up with blisters—but then the key gave way before my fear-driven strength. Maybe it was adrenaline, or maybe it just wasn't that hard to turn to begin with and I was merely panicking, but I managed to turn the key.

The moorings dropped away, disappearing into the rapidly moving waters below. I shouted in triumph and then climbed swiftly back onto the deck.

I had to throw myself onto the wooden planks as more gunfire rang out over the sea. Glass broke, and the railing I'd just been standing at splintered into ruin, but I was unharmed by the assault.

I ran back up to the upper deck and dropped into the copilot's chair next to Will.

"It's good," I shouted. He stared over at me in disbelief, but then a grin stretched wide over his features.

"Then it's time to say goodbye to these stubborn assholes," he said with glee. He pushed the button, and this time was rewarded with the whirring vibration of the hydrofoils engaging.

We exchanged delighted smiles as the boat began picking up speed, gradually rising above the choppy waves. The ride was so much smoother, and I couldn't believe we were only touching the water with a few feet of metal on either side.

"Ha!" Will pumped his fist in the air as he beheld our pursuers dwindling into the distance behind us. "Fuck you, bunch of Russian assholes."

"How do you know they were Russian?" I asked, sinking into my seat as relief robbed me of my adrenaline rush. I was shaky with my recent exertions and the intense pressure and now felt as if I could turn into water and form a puddle under my seat.

"Just a hunch," Will said. He turned an admiring gaze upon me, and quickly pecked me on the cheek while keeping his hands on the controls. "You were fantastic, babe. I couldn't be prouder of you."

My cheeks flushed, and I started toying with my hair. Being appreciated for my body was one thing, but sincere praise just rang so much sweeter and truer to me.

"I only did what I had to," I replied as casually as I could, though I was delighted with his praise.

"Yes, but lots of folks don't do what they 'have' to. You stepped up where a lot of experienced soldiers would have faltered. You're one incredible woman, Scarlett Shaw."

I threw my arms around his neck and smothered him with kisses.

"You're only saying that because it's true," I purred.

After we finished laughing, I asked what I felt was a pertinent question.

"Where are we going to go now?" I sighed. "I mean, they obviously know this yacht. It can't be safe."

"Not to mention driving a shot-up boat is going to attract all the wrong kinds of attention," Will agreed. "I've got a place we can hole up for a while."

"What place?"

He turned to me and flashed that brilliant bad-boy smile.

"My nonna's place, of course."

His grandmother? Now I was truly shocked. But also relieved. We faced death together and came out all right on the other side, a few blisters and splinters notwithstanding.

I'd call that a victory any day of the week.

Chapter Twenty-Two

Will

AFTER OUR CONFRONTATION WITH THE RUSSIANS, something was different about Scarlett that I couldn't put my finger on. Not that she looked any different, her crimson tresses catching the rays of the dying sun and revealing other hues hidden within.

It was more subtle—the way she stood, the way she spoke. I didn't realize it at the time, but looking back I believe she had begun to think of the two of us as an inseparable unit. A sort of connection that went beyond friendship, beyond mere lovers, and scratched the surface of something sublime.

At the time, however, I chalked it up to nerves and her being a bit tired after hanging off the side of a speeding yacht over choppy ocean waves.

"Will?" she said suddenly as I steered us toward the Jersey coastline, aiming for a reed-shrouded private harbor that I hoped only I and one other person knew about.

"Yeah?" I turned my thoughtful frown on her beautiful freckled face.

"How..." She swallowed hard, her face drawn up in anxious misery, green eyes swimming with trepidation. "How long does it usually take to get ransom money put together and delivered?"

"Not long. A day or two at the most, unless someone's trying to jack you around and pretend like they can't liquefy their assets..." My voice trailed off as I realized what a dumb ass I was being. I'd just as much as said that Hunter Shaw was playing games with his daughter's life. "But that's not always the case," I backtracked, but the damage had been done. "It doesn't mean your father's problems aren't completely legit."

She nodded, but I could tell that it was too late. Scarlett remained quiet for the rest of the journey to shore. I turned our course parallel to the coast, keeping my eyes peeled for a particular outcropping, which sort of looked like an overweight man sitting on a toilet.

When I spotted it at last, the stone dark and wet from the pounding sea, I knew we didn't have far to go. We reached a secluded bay, whose inaccessibility meant it had yet to be developed. Tall reeds formed a barrier to both the wind and prying eyes. I pulled through a narrow passage between them and came upon a long, battered wooden dock.

Normally, one wouldn't tie up a million-dollar luxury yacht at such a humble place, but this was far from a normal situation. I jumped over the side and onto the dock, which creaked under my weight, and gestured toward Scarlett.

"Toss me the mooring rope," I called.

She did as I bade and then carefully stepped over once I'd tied the rope off with a double hitch. I gave it one last experimental tug to make sure it would hold and then escorted her to the marshy shore.

"Whoa," she said as we reached the end and stood in the outskirts of the woods. "Is that your nonna's cabin?"

"Yes," I said as the building came fully into view. It was pretty simple, one story with no separation between kitchen, living space, and dining area. There was a separate bedroom, but my nonna had slept there on our trips. I had fond memories of curling up in front of the fireplace on a bear skin rug, which my grandfather had allegedly shot many years ago.

"You got awful quiet, Daddy." Scarlett hooked her arm around mine.

"Just lost in a memory." I shook my head.

"Tell me," she prompted, squeezing my arm. "Pretty please?"

She batted her lashes, and I knew I couldn't look into that smiling face and deny her anything, even if she told me to drag the moon out of the night sky.

"I guess I remember falling asleep in front of the fire while my nonna knitted. Simple times, much simpler. Before I realized the kind of family I really wound up with."

I found the key inside of a red and white painted birdhouse and opened the door. It smelled a bit musty inside, but I figured opening the windows and airing it out would alleviate that problem. Nonna, even nearing ninety years of age, never left the cabin without making sure it was tidy. There was no dust, and the kitchen utensils hung neatly organized from hooks driven into the wood wall.

The cabin had the usual trappings, like a taxidermist-created big mouth bass hanging on the wall, and a gun rack with well-maintained small-caliber rifles. And of course, the aforementioned bear skin rug.

"This place is actually pretty cozy." Scarlett nodded with approval. Her eyes lit up. "Ooh, is that a fireplace? I love sitting in front of an indoor fire. I can't explain why."

"We'll make one soon enough." I took down one of the rifles and made sure it was loaded. It was. Good old Nonna. "First I need to check the perimeter and make sure we're truly alone."

"Check the perimeter," Scarlett said in a deep voice, mocking me again. "You sure talk like an action movie hero despite your many protestations to the contrary." I cocked an eyebrow at her and grinned, but her face grew somber. "Will, who were those guys who attacked us on the yacht? Did they… Did your family send them after us because you wouldn't cut off my toe?"

"I'm not sure," I replied, my smile fading. "It's not really my family's style, but where else could they have come from?"

"I don't know. My dad maybe?"

I considered it, though it seemed unlikely. It seemed to me that all Hunter Shaw would have to do, if he didn't want his daughter back, would be to not pay the ransom…

Sort of like he was doing. But I could have been wrong about his motivations.

"I doubt it, but I suppose nothing can be ruled out." I picked up the landline phone and dialed star sixty-seven so the number couldn't be traced—a trick that didn't work with modern cell phones—and dialed Devlin's number. I was surprised when he answered almost immediately.

"What the hell, Devlin?" I snapped before he'd even finished saying hello. He sighed heavily into my ear.

"Look, Will, this is the way the game is played, but I'm sorry about the toe. We can do a lock of hair if that makes you feel better..."

"This isn't about the fucking toe, Devlin," I growled low.

"Then what is it about? If you're getting tired of babysitting the girl, I can find someone else."

The thought filled me with nameless dread and nigh-on panic. "No, that won't be necessary."

"Are you sure? Because I'm starting to wonder where your loyalties lie, bro."

"Is that why you sicced your goon squad on me?" I blurted.

"Goon squad?" Devlin's voice seemed to be sincerely confused. Maybe I was wrong about him. "What in the hell are you going on about now?"

"How about six heavily armed Russians—fucking *Russians*! Why did you use them? You know they always go overboard—shooting up my boat. That ring any bells?"

Devlin's scoffing laughter bubbled up into my ear, and right away I knew I'd been hasty to accuse him. "Shoot up your… Shoot up your boat?" He gave in to another fit of lusty guffaws. "Why would I need to—never mind, I'm offended you think I'd hire Russians more than you think I'd try to have my own brother rubbed out."

"Well, you've never really acted like my brother. Have you?" I snapped. Scarlett shifted uncomfortably from foot to foot while she watched my face go through multiple emotional contortions.

"This again?" Devlin sighed. "Look, Will, she was a grown ass woman, and you were too… intense for her, all right? I'm more laid back, always have been, and we just vibed better. That's it. If you'd been paying more attention to what she was saying, what she was feeling, instead of being worried about me, it never would have happened anyway."

He didn't say a single thing that I didn't already know to be true, but still it stung.

"Well, if you didn't sic a goon squad on me, then who did?" I said at length.

"That, I don't know." Devlin's voice carried an aura of menace. "But I intend to find out. Nobody takes a shot at one of the Mayne brothers unless they're tired of life. I hope you understand that I've got your back, bro—Will."

I heaved a sigh, my anger largely deflating—both what I felt at that moment, and the anger I'd been carrying inside for many years. "Yeah. I do understand that, Devlin."

"Good. So you'll bring the girl to me so we can sort this whole thing out."

My heart skipped a beat. "No dice, Devlin."

"No dice? What do you fucking mean, no dice?" Devlin sputtered. "Did you forget the pecking order at the firm, Will? When I say jump, you say how high. You feel me?"

"Yeah, I feel you, but I also feel you don't have control of this situation any longer," I snapped back. "You didn't even know that someone attempted a hit on your own brother. So, what I said stands. No dice. I'll keep watch on her until this whole thing is settled. And that's that."

"Goddamn it, Will, I'm on your side." Devlin sighed. "Fine. I was afraid you would cop this attitude, so I took some precautionary measures."

My blood ran cold, and I instantly peered out of the window at the fading sunlight dappling the forest. It seemed peaceful, tranquil, but appearances could be oh so deceiving.

"What did you do, Devlin?" My tone low, flat.

"What I had to do, baby bro." Devlin almost sounded apologetic. Almost. "What I had to do. I'm not about to let you get shot, but I did dispatch an old friend to 'remind' you of where your loyalties are supposed to lie. Good luck."

With that he ended the call, and I slammed the receiver down hard. I exchanged glances with Scarlett and then walked over and handed her the loaded rifle.

"I hate guns, Will."

"I know you do, babe, but please, just keep it for now. I'm going to check the perimeter."

"What did he say that has you so scared?"

Silence was the only answer I could give.

Chapter Twenty-Three

Scarlett

THE MOOD IN THE CABIN GREW DARK FAST WHILE WILL had been on the phone with his brother. I sensed a great deal of turmoil inside of him, lurking behind his blue eyes as he checked another rifle while he prepared to head outside.

I didn't press him for details and instead just watched as he pushed open the door and headed into the twilight-purple wilderness. Then I turned around and sighed, regarding the rifle in my hands. What had I sunk to? Carrying the very thing I'd said I would destroy.

A thought occurred to me. Wouldn't it be ironic if…

I turned the rifle around, so the barrel pointed at the floor, and checked the stock. Yup, wouldn't you know it? A *Shaw Rifle*. It seemed like I couldn't escape my father's legacy no matter what occurred.

While Will did his perimeter check and ran around the woods feeling all manly and stoic, I looked for something to eat. The pantry yielded a lot of dried goods. Some of it I expected to find, like instant biscuit mix, but there were vacuum-sealed foil bags of milk as well.

There were a lot of dark plastic wrapped items, which had the initials MRE on them. When I read the acronym, it apparently stood for Meals Ready-to-Eat. I guessed they were military rations, which made sense if a person wanted to spend time in a cabin many miles from what some considered civilization.

My mind raced back to the events on the ocean, when those men were trying to kill us. I had been terrified, of course. How could I not be scared when people were shooting military-grade assault rifles at me? But the funny thing was, I hadn't been nearly as scared as I probably should have been.

Traveling in the suitcase, handcuffed and gagged while locked inside of the stifling trunk of Will's car, had been far, far scarier. Even though I wasn't in any immediate danger while trussed up in the trunk, it had seemed so much worse.

I considered the differences in the two situations. The biggest factor in determining my level of fear response, I believe, was my ability to act and affect the outcome. While in the trunk, helpless and tied, I couldn't do anything at all to alter my fate. But on the yacht, I was able to take action to *do* something about what was happening to me. Plus, I could breathe, and see, and didn't have to deal with my own panties trying to slide down my throat and suffocate me.

So, in the last couple of days I'd been kidnapped, trussed up like a damsel in distress, zipped up in a suitcase, carted about in the trunk of a car, and shot at on the high seas before pulling off some stunt work that would make Tom Cruise proud.

My old life, that of sitting around in cafés and making video blogs, seemed so far away. I wasn't sure if my circumstances were truly the only differences. I thought instead that perhaps it was me. I was no longer the same woman who'd gone to that rave because she wanted to look cute and dance the night away.

I was hardly a gourmet—the debacle of the burned pancakes had proven that beyond a shadow of a doubt—but I set out several boxes with the plan to create some form of meal. The instant biscuits box promised an easy dish within half an hour—literally just add water. There was a sealed can of sausage gravy which I set out next to it, and then I rummaged about for something, anything, that might resemble a vegetable.

The closest thing I could find was Borracho beans, and they joined the assembly on the counter. I started at the sound of the door opening and turned to smile at Will as he entered the cabin.

It was obvious he was feeling a good deal less tense. His brow was no longer furrowed, and his shoulders had lost the tight posture they'd held before. Will leaned the rifle against the door frame after clicking on the safety and then came across the floor to embrace me.

"I'm sorry I got a little testy," he mumbled into my hair.

"It's all right." I squeezed him tightly. His smell, tinged with humus and sweat, drove me crazy and I felt a tingle between my legs. "I take it there aren't more Russians lurking out in the woods?"

Will laughed and pulled away enough to look me in the eyes. "No, I didn't see anyone." He cupped my cheek with his calloused palm. "We're quite alone."

He moved to kiss me, but I fended him off. "Uh-uh," I waved my finger at him. "No pussy until you feed me. And don't try being cute. I'm talking about food and you know it."

He arched a brow but then burst into laughter. "All right, fair enough." He moved into the kitchen and frowned at what I'd laid out. "What is this?"

"I was going to try and cook something."

"Ah, I don't think that will be necessary."

"Will." I put my arms akimbo and glared at him. "Are you trying to insinuate I'm not a very good cook?"

His mouth worked silently, but no sound came out. That was probably the best move he could have made at the time.

"Of course not," he said at length, finding his tongue at last. "But this old wood-burning stove is tricky, so maybe I should handle the food prep this time."

I chuckled and kissed him on the cheek, getting up on my tiptoes to manage it. "Okay, nice diplomatic dodge. This time. I'll just go start a fire under the mantle while you cook, then."

"You'll need some kindling to start the fire," he called. "I'd check the clearing a stone's throw out the back door. It gets plenty of sun and the deadwood should be dried out."

"Thanks." I opened the back door. "I'll be right back."

"Scarlett, wait," he turned around and frowned.

"What?" I asked, a bit impatient. Was he going to be overprotective to the bitter end?

"Take the rifle with you," he gestured at the gun leaning next to the door.

I rolled my eyes, but I did as he said.

"Make sure the safety is off before you try firing it—not that you'll have to," he stammered.

"I know. I know," I grinned. "I'll be careful, Will."

"There's a wicker basket next to the back door you can use to carry the kindling in. In fact, there might even be some in it already and you won't have to go anywhere."

I pushed the door open and peered down to find a very empty wicker basket on the deck. "No such luck." I picked it up by the handle and slung the rifle over my shoulder like an action movie bad ass. "I'll be back in a flash."

I hummed as I headed out the back door and through a short span of woods to reach the clearing. The evening's first stars were out, twinkling merrily from a dark azure sky rapidly darkening toward black. Night insects chirred in the foliage, mixing with the mating calls of toads and bird caws as I crunched through dried out grass into the clearing.

There I found thin, dry twigs, some of them with shriveled leaves attached to the stems. I filled the basket bit by bit, moving around the clearing and humming to myself the whole time. It felt nice to be doing something so mundane, so normal. The thought that I would soon eat a delicious meal—Will was quite the cook—and then spend the rest of the evening having hot, hot sex gave me a little extra spring in my step, a little extra lilt in my voice.

I knelt next to a pile of twigs apparently swept along by flood waters into a washout—a veritable gold mine of kindling. My humming gave way to singing as I gathered it up, filling my basket to the brim.

Something hard pressed into the back of my head, and I froze.

"Don't move," a voice from behind me hissed. "Or I'll ventilate your skull."

My heart thudded a rapid tattoo in my chest, and I instinctively raised my arms in the air. "Don't hurt me, please. I'm all alone. I won't give you any trouble. I swear."

"Nice." The deep baritone laughed, and I felt the presumed gun move away from my scalp. "You lie pretty well. Where's Will Mayne?"

I started for a moment. I hadn't heard Will's last name mentioned as of that point. The man behind me took my reaction to mean something different, however.

"Yeah, I know about Will, and his nonna's cabin, and the fact that you've been sucking him off or something and his head is all twisted around. I'm here to take over babysitting you while also reminding Will where the pressure lies."

I shuddered. The idea of being removed from Will's custody and placed into that of a total stranger was terrifying.

"Stay right where you are," I heard him say. There was a sound, a shuffling sound, which may have been the stranger putting his presumed gun into a holster. Then I felt a tug on my hair, which caused me to instinctively flinch away.

"Hold still," he snapped, grabbing the back of my neck and squeezing hard. I shivered as he held a shiny metal-tipped arrow in front of my eyes. "Or you'll be breathing through a new hole in your neck."

I grimaced as he tangled the arrow shaft up in my hair, twisting it around on its horizontal axis and forming a handle with which he could control me. He wound up placing the arrow's sharp tip under my chin and used it to prompt me to my feet.

"Up." I caught a flash of him with my peripheral vision as I struggled to my feet. A big man, bigger even than Will, with rusty red skin, jet black hair with threads of gray, and glittering eyes full of the promise of violence. In that one glimpse, I realized I never wanted to give this dangerous man any reason to hurt me because I knew he would. In a heartbeat.

"Let's go," he jabbed the arrowhead into my skin almost hard enough to draw blood, but not quite. "And don't even think about screaming a warning. I'll take your larynx out before you finish drawing in enough breath."

I believed him and offered no resistance as we reached the cabin's rear door.

"Open it," he hissed through clenched teeth. I did so with a trembling hand, and then he walked me inside ahead of him.

Will turned around, his smile draining away as he beheld the two of us. He held a kitchen knife in his hand, which he flipped around so he held the blade part in a throwing position.

"Don't embarrass yourself, Will," my captor said mockingly. "We both know you can't hit shit at this distance."

Will straightened, the hand holding the knife dropping to his side. "Navajo Joe," he sneered. "I should have known they'd send you."

Chapter Twenty-Four

Will

My nonna's cabin had been invaded by a six-foot-ten-inch, three-hundred-pound Native American who also happened to hold an arrowhead to my woman's throat. Not the most auspicious of reunions with a man I always saw as an unofficial uncle.

"Navajo" Joe Barrow had been in my family's employ since before I was born, working his way up through the firm when it was still in its infancy. Joe was a special forces vet, born a little too late for 'Nam but just in time for the micro wars and regime changes during the Reagan era. If he had been born in time to go to Vietnam, the war may have gone much differently.

While every stiff in organized crime had a story about their resident boogeyman, most of the time those stories were heavily exaggerated. No one's an invincible killing machine, and I mean no one.

But Navajo Joe was one of those guys where the myths and legends blurred with reality. My father told me a story once about how Joe got into a brawl with a Ju Jitsu expert, and used a unique way of breaking free from his opponent's joint lock by biting the man's index finger off at the third knuckle.

There were other stories, most of them spun by Joe himself. Supposedly he'd been surrounded in Latin America by a thinly disguised Soviet hit squad and walked out the only survivor, albeit with multiple bullet wounds. Joe once threw a Harley at a group of bikers hassling my grandmother… It's easy to get the gist.

All of this made me very, very wary that he was here in Nonna's cabin, holding my woman hostage.

"Of course, they sent me, Mai-Koh," Joe grinned. "Everyone else was scared shitless to come after you. You've developed quite the reputation in your brief return."

"Let her go, Joe," I put the knife away as a sign of good faith. "This is between me and you."

"I'm afraid not, boy." Joe's wizened face wrinkled further with a sneer. "My business is very much with her. I'm going to take over babysitting Miss Shaw until this deal is done. I only returned because I wanted to tell you as much to your face. I hate the idea of you running 'round the woods keening like a baby because you lost her."

"Come on, Joe." I spread my arms. "You know me. Would I do something to endanger the firm?"

"Not unless you didn't know any better," Joe snorted. Scarlett yelped when he yanked on her tangled hair, driving the arrow point deeper into her skin but not quite piercing her flesh. "This is a pretty little white girl you've got here. I'm sure she's got your mind all twisted up with bad medicine. Fortunately for you, the Shaman is here to dance away your demons."

My eyes narrowed and I took a step forward. "You're not leaving here with her, Joe."

"Will, please, I'll be fine," Scarlett pleaded with me.

"Not now, Red," I pushed from behind clenched teeth.

"I don't want you fighting your own family because of me," she pressed. Joe tilted his head back and laughed, feather tokens in his hair dancing with his mirth.

"Your woman has more sense than you do, Mai-Koh." Joe jutted his chin toward the door. "I'll give you one last chance to walk away."

I turned my head to the side, a bit confused. "Wait—you want to hold her here?"

Joe shrugged. "Why not? It's as good a place as any, and the only people who know where it is are you, me, and Iris."

Joe had always called Nonna by her first name. There was probably some history there—how else would he know how to find this place?—but I didn't have time to unravel it now.

"It is a good hideout," I said at length. "How about we make a deal, Joe?"

His gaze narrowed, and he jerked Scarlett about and forced her to kneel painfully at his feet. "I don't make deals, boy. You should have figured that out a long time ago."

"I know, but you'll like this one, I think," I said quickly. "How about if you hang out here with us until the ransom comes through? That way you're still doing your job, right?"

"Hmm." Joe seemed to consider the offer but then shook his graying head. "No go, boy. Devlin insisted I handle this personally and *alone*. If I don't, it might hurt my rep. You know how it is."

Navajo Joe was incredibly loyal to the family as a whole, if not its individual members. I didn't know why, but he was. His story about his rep had nothing to do with things. He just didn't want to disappoint the family.

"All right." I held up my hands. "I can see you're not about to make any deals. But what about a bet?"

"Bet?" Joe's brows rose. He might have been the Native American Superman, but Joe's kryptonite was gambling. It was the only reason he hadn't retired yet, when he was compensated better than many corporate CEOs, tax free I might add. "What's your bet?"

"I bet that I can take you out, hand to hand, no weapons…" My voice trailed off as Joe was overcome with great peals of laughter. His eyes squeezed tightly shut, moisture forming at the corners as he gave in to his mirth.

"I'm sorry, boy. What were you saying?" Joe made a show out of cleaning out his ear. "I could have sworn that you just said you could take me out."

"That's exactly what I said." I crossed my arms over my chest. "If I beat you, you take your leave and let me continue to perform the task I was assigned. If you win, you take the girl."

Scarlett shot me a dark look, probably not fond of the idea of being a "prize" in a fist fight between two old frenemies. But she didn't understand that we had very few options.

"Huh. You've got balls, Mai-Koh." Joe dragged Scarlett to her feet and pulled her over to the cabin wall. With a powerful, short thrust of his arm, he drove the arrowhead two inches deep into the timbers, pinning Scarlett in place.

Then he stepped back to the center of the cabin and doffed the camo jacket he wore, revealing a black tank top beneath. His muscular arms and chest belied his age, and he moved as spryly as a twenty-year-old as he loosened up.

Shit. This was the part of the plan that might hit a snag—beating the old Navajo bastard in a fair fight. I wasn't sure I could beat him in an *un*fair fight. But one look at the terrified red-haired woman made me realize I had no choice.

I stepped toward him, raising my arms in a classic boxer's defense and turning my body slightly to the side. Joe didn't lift his hands, keeping them down by his sides. I didn't take the bait. I'd sparred with him enough times to know he liked to bait his opponents into taking the offense.

"Your jabbing arm is dipping beneath your shoulder," Joe pointed out as we circled each other in the living room floor. "That's going to cut down on your power."

"Should you really be giving me advice?" I snapped, though I did adjust my stance.

"Sure," Joe shrugged. "How else is this going to be any fun whatsoever?"

I stepped forward and launched an exploratory jab, trying to find my range. Joe still didn't lift his hands into a guard. He simply bobbed and weaved out of the way of my offense. A slight smile tugged at the corners of his mouth. I didn't want to let him get inside of my head—at least half the game was mental—but his arrogant attitude grated on my last nerve.

"All those pumped-up beach muscles, and that's the best you've got?" he taunted as I drove him back. I had him on the run, at least, bobbing and dodging under my onslaught. My anger got the best of me, and I swung for the fences rather than continue the measured, careful assault I had been launching.

Which meant I fell right into his carefully laid trap. Joe sidestepped an overhand right roundhouse punch and cracked me hard across the jaw with a counter punch. My vision grew dark at the edges, and I stumbled forward onto my knees.

I was barely able to duck underneath a well-aimed kick, his boots smacking the ends of my hair. It was that close. If he'd connected, I would have been out for hours, maybe days.

Curling my body, I pitched into a somersault and came up on my feet, a trick I'd learned in the service. Joe whistled as if impressed.

"Not bad, not bad at all," Joe chuckled. "You'll have to teach me that little bit of tumbling when you wake up."

I was too dazed to engage in verbal scuffling. I was having enough trouble with the physical sparring. Except this was no practice match. It was a high-stakes gamble, a fight with Scarlett's life on the line. While I had no proof that she wouldn't be safe with Joe, I didn't want to take the risk, either.

Joe moved forward, and I managed to land a pretty solid shot to his breadbasket. He flinched, hand clutching the impact site. That was the location of one of his old gunshot wounds.

"Fighting dirty, eh kid?" he snapped. Then his grimace turned into a bright smile. "That's my boy! I feel like I can stop holding back with you now."

"Oh shit," I cursed as he raised his hands at high angles, a classic Muay Thai position. He drove me backward with stiff kicks to my inner thigh, which I couldn't quite evade. The pain of being hit in that spot is excruciating. It's also a potentially lethal blow if it ruptures the femoral artery.

I was almost back against the stove. Out of options, I did what I had to do.

I cheated.

Reaching back, I grabbed the old-school cast iron skillet by the handle and whipped it forward. Joe saw the blow coming and crossed his arms over his face, but I still smacked him hard enough to send him stumbling back.

I pressed my momentary advantage, surging forward and swinging the skillet again. But Joe's hand snapped out and caught the edge, stopping my attack in its tracks.

"Is it my turn now?" He flashed a sneering grimace.

He punched out with the skillet, whose handle I still held. So great was his strength that he hit me right in the forehead anyway, despite my efforts to stop the blow. He did so two more times before I collapsed onto the floor.

"You're one dirty fighting son of a gun, Will," Joe spit onto the floor as he rubbed the sore spot where I'd hit him with the pan. "I couldn't be prouder. But it's time for you to learn why they call me the slayer of white men."

He raised the pan up over his head, and I wondered if maybe this really was the end.

Chapter Twenty-Five

Scarlett

My scream cut through the fire-warmed cabin air as Joe towered over Will, the frying pan wielded like a club in his meaty fist. I'd been struggling to disentangle my hair from the arrow thrust firmly into the cabin wall ever since they started brawling, but at that precise moment my efforts took on a new urgency.

The arrowhead had been buried between two timbers and then twisted sideways, so it wasn't a matter of simply pulling it out. I had to twist it as well, which was nearly impossible with the short span of tresses between my scalp and the arrow.

Reaching back over my head, I grabbed the arrow shaft in a two-fisted grip and yanked hard, teeth gritted against the strain. My efforts were rewarded by a sharp crack of wood. Suddenly I realized that all I had to do was break that shaft and I'd be free.

My mouth flew open in a scream of rage and frustration and the wood shaft yielded at last, splintering in two. I was up to my feet instantly, grabbing for the closest weapon I could find. My fingers closed around the handle of a cold iron fire poker, a heavy one with a baseball-sized stylized knot right before the ashen hook.

With a grunt of exertion, I swung the poker with all my might at the back of Joe's head. Because of our height difference, the baseball-sized knot hit him rather than the pointed end. The impact was tremendous, wrenching the tool out of my grasp. I groaned in alarm and stared at my suddenly numb limbs, which could barely make fists at that moment.

Joe stiffened when I hit him with the poker, but he didn't go down. The towering Native American pivoted about, with considerably less grace than he'd displayed so far. His eyes were full of shock rather than anger, and I wasn't sure he was completely conscious or aware of his surroundings.

But he was aware enough. He took a step forward, lifting the frying pan up over his head. Joe was going to kill me before he toppled over himself. I was certain of it. I took a reflexive step back and cried out at the top of my lungs. "Will!"

He stirred, rising to his hands and knees and shaking the cobwebs out of his head, but I knew he'd never make it in time to save me.

I threw my arms up over my head and shrank back against the very wall I'd been pinned to with the arrow. But the expected blow didn't come. I opened my eyes, peeking from between my fingers, and I saw Joe swaying unsteadily on his feet. A line of blood trickled down his forehead and ran to the tip of his nose, looking like ghastly war paint.

The frying pan dipped toward the floor, his grip slowly loosening as his eyes fluttered closed.

Then those fierce eyes snapped open, and his face contorted in rage. I screamed as Joe took a step forward—

—and collapsed face-first onto the cabin floor. The skillet bounced heavily once off the floor and then rattled to stillness.

Only then, when the danger had passed, did I completely break down and sob. I drew my legs up against my chest and hugged myself, rocking slowly. Somehow, Joe preparing to murder me with a frying pan was absurdly more frightening than the men shooting at us on the open seas.

I suppose it was because the danger was more immediate. I couldn't even see the bullets, but I could certainly see Joe's massive frame and the murderous iron skillet he wielded.

Then Will was there, crouching on the floor before me. He petted my head and told me it was going to be all right. He gathered me up into his arms in a fierce hug, and I clung to him like he was a life preserver in a storm-tossed ocean.

"It's all right, Scarlett," he soothed, holding me close. "It's all right."

"I thought he was going to kill you," I sobbed. "Kill me."

"But he didn't. Did he? Thanks to you, we're both still alive."

He calmed me and helped me sit in one of the kitchen chairs. Then he handed me a cup of tea he'd brewed while I was out gathering kindling, which I received with trembling hands.

While I sipped tea and regained my faculties, Will carefully checked on Navajo Joe. Once he was certain that the big man was no threat, or perhaps still alive, he folded up a bath towel and carefully lifted Joe's head, resting it on the towel like a pillow. Then he rolled the unconscious Native American over onto his side.

"What are you doing?" My voice was plagued with a tremble and weaker than I'd have liked.

"Putting him in the recovery position," Will murmured. "He'll probably be all right, though I'm sure you gave him a concussion."

Part of me wanted to say "good," but then I remembered I was supposed to be better than people like my father.

"Do we need to call him an ambulance?"

"No," Will shook his head. "Joe knew the risks when he came out here, and besides, I've seen him walk away from worse. He's going to be okay. And anyway, his pride is going to be stung enough after this without adding the indignity of waking up in a hospital."

Will placed a bottle of whiskey in Joe's open, nerveless hand and then checked his pockets. He came up with a pocket knife, which he replaced, and a cell phone, which he did not. Will cycled through the various screens, his blue eyes intense as they stared at the screen.

At length he set it down on the table next to me with a grunt of frustration.

"Damn. I should have known that an old pro like Joe wouldn't leave anything useful on his unsecured cell." He sighed. "It's all coded. I can decipher some of it, but Joe's very good at being subtle."

"Yes, it was very subtle when he tried to murder both of us with an iron skillet," I mumbled bitterly.

Will frowned but didn't admonish me. Instead he turned about to pour himself a cup of tea. I idly glanced at the cell phone, the screen of which had not gone dark yet. It was on a contacts list, the last thing Will had been scanning.

My eyes widened when I saw a contact listed as capital R, and a heart emoji. I picked up the cell phone and stared at the number, realizing I recognized it.

"What's up?" Will asked as he turned back around, steaming cup of tea in his big hand.

"This contact?" I held it up. "I know exactly who it is."

"Exactly?" He tilted his head to the side, skepticism in his features. "It's a New York area code, and that's all I can narrow it down to. I mean, there's not even a name."

"There doesn't have to be," I grinned, glad to be the knowledgeable one for a change. "R heart. Robert Hart, a lawyer employed by my father who never seems to make it into court, if you catch my drift."

"A fixer?" Will's eyes perked up, and he came over to lean his arm on the table and read over my shoulder. I enjoyed his presence so close to me. "Wait, this can't be right. Are you sure it's the same guy?"

"Yup." I nodded firmly. "I've seen the number pop up on my dad's phone for the last ten years. It's definitely the same number."

"Doesn't mean it's the same guy."

I gasped and looked up at him like he was an idiot. "R. Hart?" I sputtered. "Come on, Will. It's him. Do I have to call the number and prove it to you?"

"No," Will's glower faded as he shook his head. "I believe you. And we wouldn't want to tip him off that Joe's been compromised anyway. I just couldn't accept what's going on here at first."

"What's going on?" I asked, my face twisting into a concerned frown. Will seemed upset all of a sudden, and he was such a cool customer that it was quite unsettling and made *me* upset.

"Think about it, Scarlett," he spoke softly, the color draining out of his face. "A cleaner used by my family just happens to have your father's fixer on his contacts list? I can only think of two possible explanations, and I don't like either."

I turned toward him and rested my hand on top of his defined forearm. "Tell me, please, because I'm really scared."

He put his hand on top of my own and squeezed before continuing. "Possibility number one: Joe is not as loyal as my family thinks and has been pulling strings for your father this entire time."

"I can see where you'd find that unsettling."

"Except, it makes no sense. No offense, but your father doesn't have anything that would tempt Joe. He's not motivated by money, never has been."

Will chuckled darkly. "I think he likes the excuse to hurt people, and his loyalty to my family lets him excuse it under the guise of duty and obligation."

"Okay," I said carefully, "so you don't seem to think possibility number one is a good fit. What about possibility number two?"

Will sucked in a deep breath and stroked his chin in thought. "Possibility number two: Devlin trusts Joe more than me."

"So?" I asked when he didn't elaborate. "What does that have to do with anything?"

Will's eyes glittered as he spoke. I could tell he was thinking out loud as much as explaining. "Yes, it's all clear," he said eagerly. "Devlin didn't allow me to make direct contact with the client who ordered your abduction because he still doesn't trust me. But he did trust Joe." I laughed. "Joe does a lot of that because he's intimidating even over the phone. Leads to a lot less clients trying to screw us over."

"But how can we be sure?" I asked, suddenly connecting the dots in my mind. "What if Hart is handling the ransom negotiation for my father, and that's why Joe has his number? Maybe he was supposed to send my dad proof of life?"

"Maybe," Will's brow furrowed. "That's an excellent point, Scarlett. I should have thought of it. Unfortunately, there's only one way to find out."

He picked up the phone and tapped the call button, holding his finger to his lips.

The call was in speaker mode, so I heard Hart's familiar voice. "Have you got my money yet? That toe should have loosened him up some."

My heart jumped into my throat, and Will ended the call. When our gazes met, I knew he realized my panic at the sound of a voice I'd heard since childhood.

"What are we going to do?" I rasped.

"We're going to go unravel this at the source." Will's voice was grim. "We're going to talk to your father. Now."

Chapter Twenty-Six

Will

THE SUN SANK BELOW THE HORIZON, CASTING THE marshy woods into darkness broken only by silver shafts of moonlight wafting through the canopy. Scarlett and I picked our way carefully through the woods, keeping to firmer ground as best we could.

Scarlett was a natural, picking up on the overland travel technique quickly. She automatically scanned ahead for patches of ground bearing clumpy vegetation or rocky surfaces. I was impressed because I'd seen soldiers in the field who never really quite learned the technique.

Fortunately, we were not overly concerned with moving quietly. It was a long, slow walk, and it took nearly two hours just to cover three miles of terrain and reach the highway. Along the way, Scarlett and I spoke about the nighttime sounds, how peaceful the woods were, and pretty much anything other than the fact it appeared increasingly likely that either a close associate of her father's was behind the kidnapping, or perhaps Hunter Shaw himself.

"Look at that." She paused to point her freckled arm at a spectacle happening in a copse. A mockingbird flashed its white striped wings as it pursued a squirrel about, chirping madly the whole time.

On occasion, the squirrel would stop and turn as if it wanted to fight, but the cagey mockingbird wasn't having any of it. We both laughed as the bird successfully drove the fluffy-tailed rodent away and then flew up to perch upon a branch, puffing its chest out like a conqueror.

"On paper, a two-ounce bird versus a three-pound rodent doesn't seem like a fair fight," Scarlett chuckled.

"It's not always the size of the dog in the fight. It's the size of the fight in the dog." I gave her a wry grin. "You weigh two hundred pounds less than Navajo Joe, but he's the one laid out in the cabin."

She shook her head dismissively as we continued on our trek toward the highway. "Yeah, sure, I'm a real bad ass when I sneak up on someone and hit them over the head when they're not looking."

I laughed and stepped over a wide expanse of boggy creek. Then I offered my hand to Scarlett to help her across. When she stepped down on the other side, our bellies wound up tightly pressed together.

Our eyes met, and then by mutual unspoken agreement, so did our lips. We broke it off before it got too heavy—we had a lot to do before morning—but it was intense enough that she giggled and patted my growing erection.

"Sorry, Big Bad Wolf. You'll have to wait to ravage Little Red Riding Hood until later."

"Are you sure about that?" I asked with a low growl.

"Pretty sure." She twirled her hair around her finger. There were still bits of arrow shaft tangled in her crimson locks, so I picked them out. Her face grew suddenly serious. "Will, what if my dad *is* behind the kidnapping? What am I supposed to do?"

I grew tight-lipped because I had no real answers. When I felt even a minor betrayal by family, it made me run and join the armed services. I can't imagine what it might feel like to have your parents willing to sacrifice your very life for their financial gain.

"We'll burn that bridge when we come to it," I finally said at length, and she graced me with a smile, though the darkness quickly returned. "As of this moment, all we have is an unproven theory. Maybe it'll turn out this is all a big misunderstanding."

I didn't believe a word of what came out of my mouth, and I knew Scarlett didn't either. But she had the good grace to nod in agreement, giving lip service to my unsubstantiated theory.

We reached the highway at last and hiked a half mile to a gas station. There I borrowed the clerk's phone and used a ride service. In order to keep us from having a paper trail—though I suppose these days it should be called a digital trail if one is being literal—I had the clerk pay with his credit card and handed him a hundred dollar bill, which was three times the proposed fare cost.

The car arrived, driven by a delightfully mundane fortyish single mother who wasn't feeling especially chatty, which suited my mood perfectly. It suited Scarlett's mood as well. I could tell that the closer we got to confronting her father, the more upset she became.

When the glittering skyscrapers of Manhattan loomed in the windshield, Scarlett reached over and clutched tightly at my hand. I dragged her over into my embrace, and she leaned her head on my shoulder and silently wept. My heart felt a cold stab of sympathetic misery, and I vowed right there that no matter what, I would make sure no one ever made Scarlett cry ever again.

"You okay back there?" called the driver, concern knitting her already furrowed brow.

"We're fine, thank you," Scarlett sniffled a bit and wiped her tears.

The driver took us to Brooklyn and dropped us off at a self-serve storage depot. Scarlett stood very close to me, shuddering. It wasn't the nicest of neighborhoods, which was why the storage depot was protected by an eleven-foot-high fence topped with barbed wire. Some scraps of clothing and a red stain on one of the fence posts told the tale that even a daunting fence wasn't always enough to keep out the urchins, but it was better than nothing.

I used my card to swipe the gate open, and then we walked inside hand in hand.

"What are we doing here?"

"I need to pick up some things for our op," I murmured.

"Our up?" she questioned, her lips pursed. "What are you talking about?"

"Not our *up*," I said with emphasis. "Our *op*. Short for operation."

"Oh, I love it when you talk all military." She flashed me a grin, but darkness still lurked within her emerald gaze. Until we resolved the issues between her and Hunter Shaw, she would know no peace.

I took a moment to think about how crazy the last few days had been. When this all started, Scarlett had been merely a job. Sure, I thought she was hot, but I usually didn't allow my personal taste to interfere with my professionalism.

But the only problem was, when it came to Scarlett, my Little Red Riding Hood, professionalism went right out the window. I knew from almost the moment I laid eyes on her that I was in danger of getting emotionally involved. The fact that Scarlett was not a vapid, brain-dead heiress but an intelligent and creative soul with ambition only made it that much harder.

Then there was her hard-luck story, common ground we had by not getting along with our families. Yeah, I didn't stand a chance, really. The fact that she looked like a goddamned Victoria's Secret model was more incidental than some might think, but it certainly didn't hurt matters.

We strode through the parking lot to my storage unit, passing under a buzzing streetlamp awash in swarming insects. A black bat darted through the cloud of bugs, zipping with grace and speed as it gobbled them up wholesale. I wondered if Scarlett and I were the bat in the current situation, or the insects waiting to be devoured.

I stopped in front of the orange corrugated garage-style door labeled #66 and dug out my key. Once I'd convinced the stubborn, rusted lock to open, I bent over, grabbed the handle, and yanked upward.

"Holy shit." Her eyes went wide, mouth forming an O as she beheld the largest and most expensive item in the storage unit—my orange and black 1962 Triumph Spitfire. The chrome gleamed in the half light as she moved inside the unit and ran her hands over the glossy polished hood. "This is awesome." Scarlett turned back toward me, her face drawn up with suspicion. "Are you *sure* you're not James Bond?"

I laughed and flipped on the lights, revealing several industrial metal shelves filled with neatly organized boxes. "I would never be caught dead in a tux outside of my wedding day."

"Are you dropping hints?" Scarlett asked hopefully. When she saw my astonished, gaping face, she laughed. "Calm down, Will. I'm just teasing." Her expression darkened, and tension stiffened her posture. "We have to survive the next twenty-four hours before we even think about the future."

I set down the box I had been about to open and went to her, gathering her in my arms. "Hey, hey," I murmured as she stiffened in my grasp. "It's all right. We're not going to die."

I left out that someone would probably end up dead even if it wasn't either of us. I was trying to be comforting, after all.

Once I had her calmed, I dug around in the box until I found what I'd been searching out—a pair of dangling diamond stud earrings with a hidden feature. They were what we used to call "bugs" in the parlance of our family business. I would be able to listen in and hear everything Scarlett and her father said to each other.

Of course, Scarlett had no idea of any of this when I handed them to her, placing them in her soft palm.

"Is now really the time to accessorize?" She quirked a red brow.

"They're listening devices," I replied. "Set up to feed into this burner cell phone. We can record everything you and your father say and play it back at will."

Scarlett nodded and removed her golden studs to replace them with the diamonds. Then we climbed into the Spitfire and made our way out of town. Like a lot of rich types, Hunter Shaw only had his business address in the city. His home was about five miles out, occupying a rocky twenty acres and featuring its own private drive.

When we reached the end of the private drive, Scarlett got in the driver's seat and I prepared to hike across the manor grounds in a black sweatshirt and hood.

"You look more like a kidnapper than ever," she chuckled.

"Be careful, Scarlett," I replied, pausing to kiss her deeply. "Try to give me at least five minutes to make it into position."

"Position," she giggled. "I'm sure there's going to be all kinds of 'positions' once you get me back to your place."

I kissed her again, and then we parted ways. The terrain was a bit rough, but also featured plenty of cover. I made it up to the house without incident, spotting Scarlett parking the car in the circle drive.

I grew up with affluence, but Shaw's manor was still pretty impressive. Four stories, a grand ballroom on the ground level just past the entrance foyer, and polished marble floors. There was a shooting gallery built into the back yard, set up so a rocky rise would absorb the rounds fired.

I tried to imagine Scarlett growing up here, but I just couldn't picture her as anything but a—very busty—adult woman.

Hunter had a thug on guard duty, a muscle-bound oaf who looked like he took protein shakes intravenously. He didn't concern me at all, as he was easy to avoid. Besides, guys with beach muscles weren't nearly as dangerous as they looked. They had to give up a lot of strength to be so defined.

I tracked Scarlett's progress through the house and wound up crouched in the shrubbery under her father's study window. As soon as the door opened and they saw each other, I knew Hunter Shaw was behind the whole thing. There was surprise in his eyes to be sure, but he didn't seem like a man who had just recovered the precious daughter he'd been worried sick about.

No, not at all. Frustration and rage boiled up in his gaze, not relief.

"Dad," Scarlett said at length when he stood staring at her in silence. She ran to him, threw her arms around his waist, and hugged him tightly. Hunter made no move to return the embrace, however, and she pulled away, a hurt expression in her green eyes. "What's wrong? Aren't you happy to see me?"

In response Hunter turned his back on her and walked over to the far wall of his study, right next to the window I peered through. He reached up and messed with something I couldn't see as he spoke.

"No, I'm not happy to see my pinko liberal hippie offspring, who is fully intent upon bankrupting me and destroying the family business," he snarled. "I tried to handle this by proxy, I really did, but if you want something done right…"

Hunter turned, and he had an elephant gun in his hands. A fucking *elephant gun*.

I prepared to spring into action, abandoning all stealth. No one was going to hurt Scarlett ever again.

Chapter Twenty-Seven

Scarlett

"Dad, what are you doing?" I blurted, stepping back quickly in a panic. My heart thudded so heavily I feared it would crack my ribcage and pop out onto the floor. Somewhere in the back of my mind, I screamed, *Where is Will?* at the top of my mental lungs.

Deciding I was too scared to wait for his arrival, I turned to run, but as soon as I reached for the knob, the door to the study flew open and Tharpe Saucer blocked my way with his massive body. Bigger even than Will, I cringed back from my father's guard's mere presence. I was trapped between the two of them.

"You're going to shoot me, Dad?" I snapped, my fear fueling my sudden anger. "In your own house? How are you going to spend all your money from a prison cell?"

"Prison?" my father's lined face drew up into a cruel sneer. It shamed me that I could see my own face in his, especially the nose and the brows. I didn't want to have inherited anything from that psychopath. "Prison? You think men like me go to prison? I golf with the fucking district attorney! I contributed to the election campaign of three quarters of the sitting judges in the entire city. I'm not going to prison. Now or ever."

His sneer changed into a pitiless smile.

"Besides, no one's going to find your body. The kidnapping is well-documented. I assure you I can sound sincerely miserable and terrified upon cue. You're just going to disappear, Scarlett. No one's ever going to find your body, but don't worry, I'll be sure to name a wing of the Shaw Munitions Museum after you."

"Don't you fucking dare," I snapped. The idea of him using my death to "honor" everything I'd ever fought against turned my stomach. "How can you be like this? Doesn't family mean anything to you?"

"Oh, so now you want to talk to me about family, Scarlett?" he growled, gripping the gun tightly in his fingers. "Family is supposed to look out for each other. Is that what you're saying?"

I bumped into Tharpe as I backed away, and he grabbed me by my arms. I knew I couldn't escape his iron grip, and I fervently checked the window. I nearly collapsed in relief when I spotted Will peering in. He held his finger to his lips and then disappeared from view. I decided to try and keep my father talking to stall until Will could take action.

"That is what I'm saying, yes," I replied.

"Well, then why have you spent the last five years of your life—living on my dime, I might add—trying to bring down the very thing that gave you such a fat trust fund? Huh? Why are you trying to destroy the family legacy? If family is so damn important to you."

His words hit me like a blow, and I flinched in kind. Tears welled in my eyes as I struggled to reconcile this angry monster before me with the man who taught me to tie my shoelaces. Then I remembered… the nanny taught me how to tie my shoes. Dad was always busy. I guess he was always an asshole, and I just didn't want to admit I knew as much.

"Nothing to say, huh?" he snapped. "Yeah, your tears don't mean a goddamn thing to me. You're so like your mother. She was always riding my ass, too." My mouth dropped open, and he snarled, jabbing the gun in my direction. "Don't you dare think that! Your mother's death was an accident. Unlike yours." His eyes grew suddenly cold, and his mouth closed. He was done talking. "Put her against the west wall, Tharpe," my father spoke as if he were ordering a Caesar salad. "The masonry is cheaper to replace on that side of the room."

The sound of breaking glass heralded Will's arrival. He landed in a low crouch, but then sprang in an instant, stretching out his body like a pouncing jungle cat.

He drove his shoulder right into my father's midsection, folding the older man in half. Tharpe released me in order to draw the automatic pistol he always kept in a holster at the small of his back. I assaulted him with my nails, raking bloody lines down his face.

Tharpe stumbled backward, temporarily blinded, and I used the opportunity to snag the pistol right out of its holster. When he opened his hate-filled eyes, he saw the barrel of his own weapon pointed at him.

"You didn't even take the safety off," he said, bluffing, because I knew damn well I had.

"Think so?" I asked with a sneer. "Then take a step, Tharpe. I fucking *dare you*."

I backed away until I was near the spot on the floor where Will had put my father into a choke hold. Will's muscles strained as he altered his grip.

"Say good night, Hunter," he snapped.

"No, Will," I put my hand on his shoulder. "Don't kill him."

"But he deserves it, Scarlett." His voice trembled with rage.

"Yeah, he probably does, but we're better than him. Aren't we?"

It came out as more of a query than the statement I'd intended, but Will released my father. Then he squatted down next to him and played the recording of his confession. Every. Single. Word.

"I've got your ass," Will informed my father. "Confessing to felonies galore. One hair comes to harm on Scarlett's head, and you'll beg me to let you die. Understand?"

My father is many things, but he's not stupid. He nodded his agreement, but that wasn't good enough for Will. The massive Wolf's hand encompassed my father's throat.

"I want to hear you say it."

"I understand," my father croaked out in a strangled voice. "I won't hurt her, I swear."

"Good." Will released him and snarled down at him. "Call the firm and tell them everything. *Everything*. Or I'll be back when you least expect it."

Will came over to me and took my hand. Together we left the manor. We were all the way outside before I realized I was still holding the gun, which I tossed away in disgust.

We clambered into the Spitfire, Will in the driver's seat, and I turned toward him. "What happens now?"

"We pay a visit to Devlin," Will said flatly. "And put this whole thing to bed once and for all."

We drove in silence back into the city. My mind roiled with my father's attempt on my life. The only solace I had was the knowledge that Will loved me, and I loved him. In order to break away from my past, I embraced my future.

My future with the man I loved, the same man who kidnapped me and threw me in his trunk a few days ago. Yeah, it sure seemed like a spy novel plot to me.

Devlin's condo was on the Upper West Side, ironically in the same building as mine. I shook my head as Will was about to buzz Devlin and used my card to get us inside instead.

Then we rode up to the penthouse—of course he lived in the penthouse—and walked right in without knocking. For a crime lord, Devlin left his doors suspiciously unlocked.

"Knock, knock, motherfucker," Will growled as we burst in. The apparent Devlin—sitting on a tastefully upholstered divan in a white bathrobe, eating bonbons—I shit you not—looked up with surprise but no fear.

"Well, well, I was wondering when you'd show up, brother," Devlin said. "Joe has a concussion, by the way. I'm taking his medical bills out of your fee."

"Don't you brother me," Will snarled, moving over to slap the tray of bonbons out of Devlin's hand.

"Dude," Devlin said with a frown. "Not so loud. You'll wake my wife."

"I could give a fuck," Will snarled, though I noted it was in a much softer tone and lower volume. "Listen to this and tell me we weren't being played the entire time."

Devlin listened while Will played back the recording he'd made. Then both of us told the story of the last few days, though neither of us mentioned our blossoming relationship.

Though I could tell Devlin had already guessed the parameters of our association. He kept eying me craftily while Will spoke.

"All right," Devlin said. "I'll admit, Hunter Shaw played us all for fools. That will be the last mistake he ever makes…"

"No." Will glanced over at me. "Hunter Shaw gets to live. Believe me, he's learned why you don't mess with Mayhem Brothers, LLC."

I covered my mouth with my hand to hide my smile. Did he make a *faux pas* while trying to say "Mayne Brothers," or was it deliberate? In either case, it made Devlin smile as well.

"Then so be it. Your handling of this rather arduous situation has earned my trust, little brother. The contract is cancelled, and Miss Shaw is free to go."

Will and I hugged each other tightly as my heart soared with joy.

"Not that she wants to go anywhere," Devlin quipped as he sipped his tea. "Welcome to the family, Scarlett Shaw."

Will nearly fell over himself with happiness. I guess Devlin's seal of approval meant a lot to him. All I knew was I could finally let myself be happy with the man I loved. Our lives might not have fit into the parameters of a fairy tale, but at least we had our happy ending.

Chapter Twenty-Eight

Will

"Welcome to my humble abode." Smiling, Scarlett slid the key into the lock, and then opened her apartment door. We stepped inside and she did a little curtsey, waving one hand at her living room. "It ain't much, but it's mine."

"It ain't much?" I repeated, arching one eyebrow. "This is a miniature palace."

"Says the man with a yacht and God knows how many houses."

"Safe houses."

"Yeah, *safe houses*," she laughed, doing air quotes with her fingers. "Let me just pack a bag and we can be on our way. All right?" Without waiting for me to reply, she turned on her heel and headed into what I assumed to be her bedroom. I followed after her to see a heap of clothes covering the bed, shirts and dresses littering the ground.

"Wow." Standing by the doorway, hands on my hips, I took in all that mess with one single glance. Scarlett didn't even notice. She just packed her things, picking random clothes from the floor and stuffing them inside her suitcase. Thankfully, she didn't seem to be choosy about what she gathered.

Now that we had sorted everything, we had decided to take the yacht and travel down the East Coast for a couple of weeks, and I couldn't wait to hit the road. Or, rather, the ocean. It'd be nice to enjoy ourselves without having a dark cloud hanging over our heads.

"What's this?" I asked her with a mocking tone, picking up a tie from the floor. "Have you been bringing men up into this bedroom?"

"From time to time," she threw back, teasing me. "But that's over now. I have everything I need right here." Padding her way toward me, she laid one hand on my chest and kissed me. "That tie is mine anyway. I like the preppy look, ya know?"

"Huh," I muttered, "and here I was, thinking I could use it to tie you up."

She froze, her lips curling into a smile. "Well… we're not running late. Are we?"

"Not at all," I replied. "In fact, we have all the time in the world." Returning her smile, I closed the distance between us and wrapped the tie around her wrists. "This is going to be fun."

"I like fun." Looking straight into my eyes, she smiled. It wasn't a simple smile, though. It was one brimming with wickedness, one that held all the dirty things that had to be running through her mind in that moment. Now that our feelings were no longer a secret, things would be so much easier between us.

"Then you're gonna love this," I continued, tying the other end of the necktie around the bedpost. She had her back turned to me now and looked at me over her shoulder. Her eyes were wide with anticipation, and I felt a wave of energy crash against me as I imagined all the twisted little things I could do to her. She was mine now. I knew it—and so did she—but I wanted her to *experience* it.

I took one step to the side and, even though she tried to follow me with her gaze, the angle I was at stopped her. Knowing I was in her blind spot, I took off my belt, purposefully making the buckle clink. Holding it in my hands, I rolled it up and took one step toward Scarlett.

"Spread your legs," I whispered into her ear, smiling as I watched her obey. To see her like this, so dutiful and eager… Fuck, what else could I want? Give me all the money in the world and I'd just set it all on fire. Nothing would ever compare to her. *Nothing*.

Slowly, I brushed the leathery tip of the belt against the back of her knee. I brushed it upward until I found the hemline of her dress, and she trembled slightly. Grinning, I grabbed at her dress and pulled on it as hard as I could, my fingers bunching up the fabric. There was the sound of it ripping, and Scarlett gasped as I tore it off her.

"I ruined it," I continued, the tip of the belt now moving up to between her legs, "just like I'm going to ruin you." The muscles in her neck moved softly as she swallowed, and I could almost feel the anxious anticipation that gripped her. No, fuck that—she was so wet that I could *smell* her anticipation.

Keeping the belt between her inner thighs, I took a moment to appreciate the way her lace underwear hugged her curves. Her black thong left little to the imagination but, at the same time, it made my mind race as I tried to imagine what lay past the veil. And her bra, the way the lace seemed to hug the perfect curves of her breasts, almost like the hands of a past lover...

Suddenly, I felt a burst of lustful rage shooting into my veins. I thought of all the other men Scarlett had been with, the assholes she must've brought to this bedroom, and something surged inside me. Even though I knew they all paled in comparison to me, I couldn't stop myself from feeling like a possessive madman.

Gripping the belt tightly, so much I could hear the crack of the leather, I cocked my arm back and whipped the belt against her ass. I did it fast but carefully, just enough to surprise her, but I made sure not to hurt her. She yelped, her ass cheeks clenching as the belt made contact, and I stared at the red mark it had left. I did it one more time, careful to thread the line between pain and pleasure, and she became so fucking wet I could see her juices drip from her thong and pool on the floor at her feet.

Dazed, I dropped the belt from my hand.

I reached for her ass and caressed the red marks on her skin, her flesh so tender and soft. "The things I want to do to you..." I whispered, my free hand sliding up her spine and all the way up to her neck. I brushed her hair over her right shoulder and leaned in, softly depositing my lips on her nape.

"You can do them all," she whispered, and even her voice seemed *wet. Wanting.* I don't know how the fuck that works, but I swear I could feel desire dripping from her words, her whole body alight with maddening lust. I thought I liked sex, but Scarlett... Fuck, she breathed sex. She *was* sex. "I'm yours, Will. You can do with me as you please."

"And I will."

I opened the clasp of her bra, but I didn't yank it off of her body. Instead, I watched as the cups drooped over her breasts, slowly revealing her milky skin and rosy nipples. With one hand on her waist, I leaned in and kissed her between the shoulder blades. I kissed her neck, her shoulders, and every inch of naked skin that I could. In my mind's eye, I remembered the first time I had laid eyes on her, and the first time our lips touched. Back then I was nothing but a single-minded predator, but even then I *knew* she was different. All it took was a kiss for me to know.

Gently, I allowed my hand to go around her waist, and my fingers fell over the dark fabric of her thong. It was completely drenched, wet to the touch, and that made my heart beat even faster. Before Scarlett, I never really cared about the enjoyment of the women I was with—although I'm pretty sure they always enjoyed themselves—but with her... her enjoyment was half the fun. I craved seeing her writhing under me, I needed to hear her moans and screams, and I was always desperate for the way she begged me to fuck her harder and harder.

Just like me, she was insatiable.

Clenching my jaw, I grabbed her thong. I was about to tear it into shreds when I realized I wanted to take my time. After all we had gone through, I wanted to slow down and appreciate every moment.

"You know I love you. Don't you?" I whispered, brushing one thumb over her lips. "You know I will always keep you safe."

"I do," she whispered back.

Love and lust swirled inside my head until they became one and the same, and I closed my eyes and kissed her neck once more. Slowly, I lowered myself, my mouth hiking down her spine. I went down on one knee and, doing it as slowly as I could, I peeled her thong down her legs. The sight of her naked ass, the pink flush of her pussy peeking from between her thighs… yeah, that set me off.

"Step back," I commanded her, directing her movements with my hands. Still with her hands tied to the bedpost, she bent by the waist and took a couple of steps back. As she did it, her pussy revealed itself to me, and my cock became so hard I half-expected it to tear its way out of my pants. "I want to taste you every single day for the rest of my life."

Laying my hands on her ass, I leaned in, my tongue slipping past her drenched lips. I brushed it over her folds, her sweet wetness making me hungry for more, and then I covered her little pussy with my open mouth. Pushing my tongue deep inside her, I gave her a good lashing, the fingers of my right hand now pressing down on her clit.

She moaned, her hips moving so smoothly I could barely notice, but that was enough for me to go crazy. Every little thing she did was enough for that to happen. Slapping her ass with my left hand, I devoured her like a wild animal tearing into its prey, her sweet juices dripping down my chin as I consumed her. I pressed my mouth so tightly against her pussy that I could barely breathe, and the plea of my lungs for air went ignored. I just kept going until her movements shed their smoothness, the frantic sway of her hips reaching a fever pitch.

Thrusting back against me, she let a string of moans escape from her mouth, and I heard the knotted tie straining against the bedpost, the wood creaking under Scarlett's pull.

She screamed.

Her voice was like poison, filtering into my brain and seeping into my body. It unleashed an onslaught of hormones into my bloodstream, and my tongue slid in and out of her drenched pussy over and over again. Her inner walls trembled for a second, and she came hard, her fluids gushing out and dripping down her legs.

"You're such a wet mess," I told her, pulling back and sucking in a deep breath. Her own breathing was ragged and uneven, and her hair fell over her shoulders like a waterfall. Reaching forward, I cupped her heaving breasts, softly pinching both her nipples to remind her we weren't done. Not yet.

"That's your fault," she managed to say, her words coming out as a dazed groan.

"It better be."

Brushing two fingers over her pussy, I brought them up to her mouth. I laid them over her lips, and then slipped them inside. Her tongue swirled around my fingers for a second, and she moaned softly, enjoying the way she tasted. Fuck, to see her doing that was almost enough for me to want to devour her again. It took all that I had not to go down on my knees and press my mouth against her drenched pussy once more. I could eat her out for hours on end and I would never get tired.

"I love it when you're dirty like this," I told her, my cock so fucking hard I could barely think straight. "I've ruined you. Haven't I?"

"Maybe I'm the one who has ruined you," she corrected me. "But I like the sound of it. I want to be ruined. Always did." There was a slight pause, and then she added, "But only if you're the one doing it." The possessive beast that lingered inside me felt appeased for a moment.

She knew exactly which buttons to push, which levers to pull. She was perfection made flesh. That made me wonder. How in the world had I gotten so lucky? What had I done to deserve a woman like her? When I asked her those questions, whispering them into her ear, her reply came without a moment's hesitation.

"You didn't do anything to deserve me," she breathed. "You just took me. One look into your eyes and I was yours. There's nothing I could have done."

"And if you could…? Would you have it any differently?"

She responded by thrusting her ass back, trapping my cock between her ass cheeks.

"What the hell do you think?" She looked at me over her shoulder, her expression one of defiant lust. I took in the brightness in her eyes, the way locks of hair tumbled over her face, and the burgundy color of her lipstick. My cock twitched then, almost as if reminding me it had urgent needs.

"I think it's time we put that mouth of yours to good use," I told her, taking the tie off the bedpost. Her wrists, though, remained bound. "On your knees."

"What if I don't want to be on my knees?" She asked me, that defiance in her eyes burning brighter. "What are you going to do about it?"

I smiled.

Moving fast, I pressed my hand against her pussy.

"You're going to get on your knees," I told her, never looking away from her eyes, "and you're going to open that pretty little mouth of yours. Then… you know what happens then. Don't you?"

"I want you to tell me."

"I'm going to get naked, and you're going to want me inside your mouth," I continued. "I won't do it, though.

You'll just watch me get harder and harder, and I'll stop you from getting your lips around my cock every time you try."

"No…" she whimpered.

"If you want my cock, you'll have to work hard for it."

"I will…" She breathed out, and she did it in such a way that it almost seemed like her heart was about to burst. There were no longer flames in her eyes. There was a fucking wildfire there, a true raging inferno. I thought I knew what lust was, but what I saw in her eyes then… it was off the fucking charts.

"Then," I finally whispered, "kneel."

Obediently, she did as she was told.

Chapter Twenty-Nine

Scarlett

My heart hammered.

I heard my heartbeat in my ears, its steady and violent thrumming driving me crazy. Still with my wrists bound, I did as I was told and got down on my knees, all my teasing defiance now forgotten. Right now, all I wanted was to obey.

Much like he promised, he unbuttoned his shirt. Going deliberately slowly, his naked skin was revealed one inch at a time, and I realized I didn't know if I'd be capable of enduring his teasing.

"Please…" The word escaped before I could silence myself. My hands shot up to his pants, my eagerness to have him stand naked in front of me too strong for me to fight off. He grabbed my bound wrists and leaned down, the devil dancing in his gaze.

"No," he said, and I could tell that he was enjoying every second of this. "You don't get to touch me. You don't get to do anything until I tell you."

"But I need…"

"You *need* to do what I tell you." Just like that, my wrists went limp and I placed my hands on my lap. If I was to get what I wanted, I needed to obey. "Good girl."

He pushed his shirt down his shoulders, and it floated to the floor, landing in a heap at his feet. Still looking straight at me, he kicked his boots off, and only then did he take his hands to his waist. With maddening patience, he pushed down the zipper, and the sight of his tented boxers was enough for my center to clench.

"You like that?" he whispered teasingly, his thumb running underneath the hemline of his boxers. Slowly—so fucking slowly—he peeled them down, freeing his massive erection, and I unconsciously licked my lips in anticipation. Pinching my inner thigh, I forced myself to remember that I had to obey. And it was a good thing I did, or else I would've already lunged, my open mouth ready to devour him. "How much do you want me in your mouth?"

"I want it more than anything," I whispered, the words just falling from the tip of my tongue. "I'll do whatever you want."

"Good." Grinning, he gripped his cock by the root. Mesmerized, I watched as he stroked his enormous length, his fingers traveling up and down his long inches. "I want you to touch yourself."

At once, I spread my legs and draped two fingers over my clit. With my eyes glued to his cock, the motion of his hand hypnotizing me, I stroked my clit almost too viciously. Subconsciously, I pushed my knees together, trapping my hand in place as I punished the little pleasure bud at the top of my pussy.

"That's it," he stroked himself faster. "Keep going."

I did as I was told, furiously stroking my clit until it felt as if my insides were on fire. Unable to restrain myself, I slid two fingers inside myself, only my thumb remaining on my clit. Flicking my wrist, I massaged my inner walls as I kept on stroking my nub. That, coupled with the sight of his hard cock, did it for me.

I pressed my legs together even harder than before, and a sudden jolt of ecstasy shot up my spine. I opened my mouth to let out a wicked moan, and that's when Will moved in for the kill. Using his free hand, he grabbed me by the hair and tipped me into him. His cock slid into my mouth easily, silencing my moan, and my orgasm grew into something monstrous and uncontrollable. I had never come that hard in my entire life.

Deep in the throes of pleasure, I bobbed my head right away, sucking and licking as if I needed to do it in order to survive. I held his cock with my bound hands, keeping it in place as I rushed my lips down to the base. Then, frantic and eager, I popped it out of my mouth and ran my tongue down his shaft. I did it over and over again, and I only stopped when Will yanked on my hair.

"On your feet," he ordered, but he didn't even let me rise by myself. He grabbed the tie around my wrists and pulled me up. And thank God for that because my knees trembled so damn hard I doubt I would've been able to stand. "You are the best thing that happened to me, Scarlett," he continued, the lust in his voice giving way to something warm and tender. I could feel the love underneath his commands, but now that love was on full display. "I've never wanted anyone as much as I want you. I think of you every waking second of every day… I love you. I want you. I *need* you."

"I'm yours," I whispered, laying my hands over his beating heart. "Now and always." Gently, he undid the knot around my wrists, and the tie fell down to the floor. He pushed me back until my knees hit the edge of the mattress, and I fell down onto the soft surface. He climbed in after me, his hard member drawing all of my attention, and my inner voice piped up once more.

Hold him, it said, *kiss him. Fuck him.*

I couldn't help but smile. It seemed that even my inner voice, which had always been against anything that involved Will, had surrendered. That was just the way it should be. Every fiber of my being needed him, and even the soft whispers hiding in the dark recesses of my mind had accepted that as the inevitable truth.

"I want you inside me," I told him, and the words sounded like a desperate plea. Maybe because they were. Instead of teasing me again, he just took my wrists and pinned them to the mattress. He lay down on top of me, his hard cock resting against my pussy, but he didn't thrust inside. Not moving an inch, he just stared into my eyes, and I could feel him putting heavy chains around my soul. Making me his for all eternity.

I wanted that.

I wanted it so bad.

Faster than he could react, I threw my legs around his waist and pulled him in. With no other option but to let himself, he slammed his hard cock deep inside me, and I arched my back as his thickness stretched me wide. Without missing a beat, he pounded into me with all the ferocity he was capable of, the mattress springs whining under our moving weight. The wooden frame slammed against the wall over and over again, and that steady and hallowed thump lulled me into a trance.

Hypnotized by my own raging lust, I tightened the lock my legs had on his hips and pushed myself off the mattress. I twisted my torso to the side and, locked in our embrace, we switched positions. The moment I found myself on top of him, I buried my fingernails into his chest, my teeth gritted as I rocked my hips. I did it hard and relentlessly, tightening my pussy around his cock as much as I could.

Rather than just letting me be a passive victim to my punishment, he grabbed my ass and started thrusting upward, the violence of his movements matching the intensity of my own.

"Fuck," I screamed out, throwing my head back and cupping my own breasts. I massaged my own flesh, flattening the palm of my hands against them, and then pinched my own nipples so hard my scream turned into a high-pitched whine. I didn't know what it was with pain and pleasure, but the line between them was tenuous.

More, I thought, *I need more.*

Changing gears, and careful to not let his cock slip out from inside me, I raised my knees up from the mattress and replaced them with my feet. Now squatting over him, I started lifting my body up only to lower it down as hard as I could, my aching pussy slamming itself down on his cock. I kept on doing it until my muscles cramped, exhaustion gripping me tightly, but I didn't let that stop me. I slowed, my body reaching its limits, but I just kept pushing ahead.

Will was more than willing to pick up the slack.

He pushed me off of him and then forced me to lie down on my stomach. I stumbled on top of the mattress, barely knowing what was happening, and then felt his fingers on my hips. He pulled on my ass and I quickly found myself on all fours. I held my breath, half-expecting him to thrust right away, but that's not what he did.

Closing in on me, he brushed his length over my drenched inner lips, coating it with my fluids, and then pulled back. I gasped as I felt the tip of his cock wandering to my ass, and my eyes rolled as I realized what he intended.

"I... I've never done this before."

"You will now."

"Fucking right I will," I breathed out, the anticipation of the act crushing all that I was. I wanted him inside me. I wanted him to use my body in the most wicked ways he could think of, and I wanted to come so damn hard that my brain would explode. I wanted all that, and I wanted it now. That's exactly what I told him.

"Patience is a virtue," he whispered, and that's when he eased himself inside me, his thick cock stretching my entrance mercilessly. For a moment, I wondered about the mechanics of it all, but it didn't take long before my body simply accepted what was to happen.

When he finally thrust fully, it felt as if my soul left my body. I could no longer feel what happened. No, the rush of sensations was too strong for my brain to process, and I simply surrendered. Time dilated around us and, in that moment, we became one.

We came at the same time, our voices blending into a chorus of sweet agony, and my entire body reverberated with ecstasy. When I finally hit the mattress, Will's seed dripping down my thighs, it was as if I floated on clouds. I was in heaven.

"I want this," I whispered, slowly turning around so that I could face him. "Every day, for the rest of our lives. Even when we're old."

"And you'll have it." He murmured. "This and much more."

Then, we said it at the same time.

"I love you."

We smiled and held each other.

Then, in the silence of the room, it finally dawned on me. After years of looking, I had found happiness. The Big Bad Wolf had swept Red Riding Hood off her feet, and he had shown her what it truly meant to be happy. What it meant to be loved.

Thanks for reading Scarlett and Will's story! Want *more* of the *Mayhem Ever After Series*? Check out **His Tinkerbelle** coming soon!

Can he claim her? Or will he have to kill her?
http://bklink.to/ht-amazon

She's got a beautiful life.

I'll gladly burn it down to save her.

She's been a thorn in my side for as long as I can remember—Belle Barrie.

With a smile that shows a sweet disposition.

And a body that invites total depravity.

Belle thought she knew my world.

Thought she could play with the big dogs.

When her boss decides to play me, she's caught in the crossfire.

Now we're talking about a full-fledged gang war.

The kind that mows down innocent bystanders.

Her life as the bargaining chip.

Everyone knows I'm ruthless.

I'm a cold-hearted killer.

My rise through the family is followed by a trail of bodies.

Yeah, some are women.

The ones who thought they could trust me.

They paid for that mistake with their lives.

Now, there's just one more debt to pay in blood.

I need to be the monster I am.

Not the man I want to be for her.

If I win, I'll have everything I ever dreamed of.

But if I do that, Belle will die.

And I'll lose the only woman I've ever loved.

http://bklink.to/ht-amazon

About the Author

Vivi Paige is the sekrit pen name of a New York Times and USA Today bestselling romance author who decided she wanted to play on the dark side of happily ever after… Join her in a sinister world of murder, mayhem, and *marriage*.

Find Vivi online at… https://vivipaige.com

———

Want a FREE romance delivered to your inbox?

She watched him kill… Will he let her walk away?

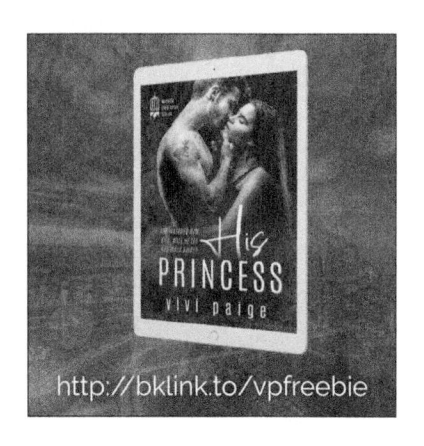

http://bklink.to/vpfreebie

Copyright © 2020 by Vivi Paige

All rights reserved.

No part of this book may be reproduced in any form or by any electronic or mechanical means, including information storage and retrieval systems, without written permission from the author, except for the use of brief quotations in a book review.

Printed in Great Britain
by Amazon

16902602R00169